Pride, Prejudice, And Curling Rocks

Pride, Prejudice, and Curling Rocks

By Andrea Marie Brokaw

Hedgie Press

Pride, Prejudice, and Curling Rocks

Andrea Brokaw

Published by Hedgie Press

ISBN: 0-9847021-0-5

ISBN-13: 978-0-9847021-0-7

Cover design by Cassandra Marshall

Author Photo by Jimmy Brokaw

Hedgie Press logo by Amanda Evans

For Jimmy,

the reason I believe in love stories

NEW SCHOOL YEAR RESOLUTIONS OF MISS DARCY BENNET

1. Graduate high school! Finally!

2. Help Jean with her resolution to have a serious boyfriend senior year. (Finally!)

3. Maintain at least a 3.5 GPA, weighted.

4. Be nicer to the half-monsters. They can't help being hyperactive six-year-olds.

5. Think of a better, if less honest, answer to "Why do you want to attend Catskill College?" than "Because it's five minutes from my curling club."

6. Win club bonspiel.

7. Win Regionals.

8. Win Nationals.

9. Become Junior Curling World Champion!

10. Win Saturday Juniors League, just for good measure.

Chapter One

It is a truth universally acknowledged that a teenage girl must be in need of peer approval, but the only peer whose approval had ever meant a thing to me was my best friend Jean. That's why I felt so betrayed when I learned my approval meant nothing to her.

College recruitment booklets were strewn across Jean's bed, testaments of her disloyalty. I stared at them in disbelief. "California? Seriously?"

My best friend wouldn't look at me as she tugged on the ash-blond ponytail draped over her shoulder. "UC San Diego has one of the strongest Oceanography programs in the world."

"Oceanography? Since when do you care about oceanography?" I picked up one of the brochures. A racially diverse group of students seemed to be having class on a beach. Like that was a good idea. Even if they managed to pay attention to the lecture, their notes would be covered in sand. "When's the last time you even saw the ocean?"

"That doesn't mean I can't be interested in it," she muttered.

I flung the ad down on top of the others and stomped over to the window. The sun slid slowly behind the Catskills, its beams tracing highlights on the fiery spread of autumn leaves. Gorgeous. Absolutely gorgeous. And after the snow came it would be even more beautiful. Why would she want to leave?

"There's no ice in California."

The springs on her bed creaked as she sat down. "Sure there is."

"Not in San Diego."

"Not outside," she said, her voice soft. "But they have indoor ice, same as anywhere."

My hands bunched into fists, fingernails digging into my palms. I leaned my forehead against the window, looking for comfort in its coolness. "There's no curling."

She sighed, loud enough that I knew she wanted me to hear it. "Yes, there is."

I shook my head, my skin rubbing against the glass. "No. There are no dedicated curling clubs anywhere near California."

"Ugh, Darcy! This is why I waited so long to tell you." There was a thump as she flopped back on the bed. "Arena ice is still ice. You can still curl on it. And it's not forever. It's just college."

Right. Only four years. Four years that would take us from our soon-to-be eighteen to twenty-two, which was a year too old for Juniors. My chest shook as I struggled to stay calm. I straightened up, but kept my back to Jean. "What happened to staying here? Going to Catskill with me? You're just going to abandon the team?"

"You know it's not like that."

Did I? I turned around and stared at her. "No, I don't know that. What I know is you're destroying the team so you can move to the opposite end of the country. And, yeah, so maybe you'll only be gone four years, but then what? You're not coming back here with a degree in oceanography. You're not going to lead us in the adult league. We're never going to the Olympics together."

"Darce..." Tears reflected in her eyes as she shook her head. "The Olympics? That was our dream when we were ten. It's not something to build a life around. Curling... It's not everything."

I blinked back tears of my own. There were so many things I wanted to say, to scream, to sob, but I didn't even know where to start. My heart was breaking and she didn't even care.

3

"Is this really about curling?" Jean asked as she sat up. Her ponytail was a complete mess now. "You don't need me to be a great curler. You'll make an excellent skip next year."

As though telling me I could take over team leadership would make me feel any better. We'd been curling together since we were eight. We'd been friends even longer. Best friends. We were supposed to be best friends forever, not best friends until college. "It won't be the same."

"No." She got up and walked to me. "But that doesn't mean it won't be awesome."

Actually, as far as I could tell, it did.

WAYS TO KEEP JEAN IN MERYTON

(or at least in New York)

1. Win Junior Curling Nationals, but not World. This will give her motive to return with us next season.

2. Write to the University of California and explain how unsuited to study the Pacific Ocean people from the Catskills are.

3. Hack into the SAT system and make it look like she failed horribly. This has the downside of keeping her out of Catskill too, but she can spend a year in community and then transfer over.

4. Convince her I will kill myself if she leaves. Though she may see through this...

5. Convince her I will kill her sister if she leaves. This is much more plausible.

6. Help her make good on that New School Year Resolution she made to have a serious boyfriend for senior year. Then let him convince her to stay.

Chapter Two

A lot of people don't understand why I love curling. They just don't get the game. They don't want to. I try not to let it bother me. I mean, it's their loss, right?

I've taken a lot of teasing for my game over the years, but it's worth it for the ends where everything clicks, when not only do you see all the right shots, but the team can come together and pull them off. The feeling of doing everything right with your best friends by your side makes up for the bad days, the ridicule, and the endless allegations that curling isn't a real sport. There's nothing that compares to the satisfaction of being down by two in the final end and scoring three to win the match. Unless maybe it's doing that in the World Championships or the Olympics or something.

I felt good about our most recent victory when we left the Catskill Curling Club, but the happy mood didn't last long into the party my teammates dragged me to afterwards.

"Come on, Darcy. Please?" Jean's eyes were huge as she clasped her hands in front of her and begged me to play wingwoman in Scarlet Johanson's living room. Normally, I wouldn't mind. I wanted to find her a boyfriend, both because it would make her happy and because if the relationship was serious enough it might keep her in-state for college. But she wanted me to distract her crush's best friend, who happened to be Lucas Fitzwilliam, who also happened to be a complete jerk.

"Why don't you go talk to Colin?" I asked. "He's been eying

you all night."

Jean dropped her hands with an exasperated grunt. "If you think Colin's so great, you go talk to him."

As it happened, I didn't think Colin was great. Adam was cuter, nicer, and much better about bathing on a regular basis. He was tall and athletic and looked a lot like he'd stepped out of the pages of one of the more dashing tales in Arabian Nights. However, Adam was also best friends with Lucas, which meant something was seriously wrong with him. Not only that, but history had shown that while Adam never had any trouble finding girlfriends, he was incredibly bad at keeping them. It made me think all his exes might know something we didn't, something that would make him not so great a catch no matter how hot he was.

"Where are Maria and Cat?" I surveyed the room, seeing neither our teammate nor her girlfriend. "I'm worried about them. They hardly know anyone here."

Jean's blue eyes rolled. "They found a dark corner somewhere. They're together, they're fine."

If they were making out in a corner, I expected some guy would've alerted us all to the hot lesbian action by then, but I had to agree they were most likely okay. I just didn't want to talk to Lucas. We shared half our classes, so I saw more than enough of him during the week.

And I didn't understand why Jean thought she needed me. It's not like she required a bodyguard on the journey across the room to the where the boys were bent over a chess board. Yes, a chess board. What kind of loser goes to a party to play chess? Well, Lucas for one. And Adam for two. What was Jean's obsession with him? Oh, right, that whole Prince of Persia thing he had going.

"Please, Darce?" Jean's chin quivered a little. Too scared to go over on her own, she was about to start crying over me refusing to help her. Dammit. I was always a sucker for tears.

"Fine."

As Scarlet's stereo blared dance music despite no one dancing, we navigated over to the boys, who sat on stools at the bar lining the far wall. Sadly, all the bottles had been removed from the bar's shelves and the only thing in the fridge Scarlet's dad had back there was pop. Alcohol might have made Lucas more tolerable, though probably not.

One glance at the board showed me Lucas was clobbering Adam. The latter reached out and put his hand on his rook, freezing when I made a little noise of disapproval. He looked up. "Not a good move?"

I shook my head. If he did what I assumed he meant to do and captured Lucas's bishop, he'd lose the rook to Lucas's queen. At this point, all he had to defend his king with was that rook and three pawns. It was possible he could force a draw without the rook, but he should try to hold onto it.

He touched the piece again and raised his eyebrows at me, seeking guidance.

"I'm not playing her too," Lucas said, crunching his face up like I was an unwanted fungus.

"Of course not," I said. "Because then you'd lose."

Adam laughed as Lucas skewered me with a look that would have made most people back down. I'd never been the kind of girl that shirks away from challenging glowers though, so I just folded my arms and glared back at him.

"Fine," Lucas said. "You're next."

While Lucas and Adam looked back at the board, Jean gave me an enormous grin. I'd been about to inform Lucas that I'd rather snack on razor blades than play a game with him, but that joyous beaming stopped the words before I could start them. Jean would owe me though. And I'd have to think of something really good to demand from her.

"So, why is this stupid?" Adam asked as he made the move I'd cautioned against. Jean's lips jerked apart to tell him, but she closed her mouth without saying anything. I ground my teeth over seeing her act dumb just so some boy didn't realize she was smarter than him. Why would she want a guy who was turned off by brains? If Adam wanted her to be the stereotypical idiot blonde, he wasn't worth bothering with.

Without comment, Lucas swept his queen over to capture

the rook. It was still theoretically possible Adam could have forced a stalemate, but he shook his head and held out his hand.

Jean inched closer to the board, frowning at it. "You're giving up?"

"Yeah, he's got me." He misinterpreted her frown for confusion rather than calculation. "He still has his queen, which can move anywhere and none of my pieces can move more than one square at a time."

She nodded like she'd needed that information. Which she most certainly hadn't. I started to think Adam had some serious problems in addition to bad taste in friends, but she kept looking at him like he was a god on earth. With a nervous nod toward the kitchen, she said, "I'm going to go grab some pizza. Anyone want anything?"

Adam took the bait instantly, jumping off the stool in his eagerness. "I'll come with." He flashed me a wink. "Kick his butt for me, would you?"

The two vanished before I could banter back and I sat down with a frown.

Pieces clicked against the board as Lucas moved them back into their starting positions. "You don't have to play if you don't want to."

"Huh?" I looked up at him. "No, I was just... Thinking about something."

He grunted and finished setting up. His hair flopped forward as he worked. It was auburn and had grown just long enough to brush his shoulders. Other girls liked his hair. If it had belonged to someone else, I may have too. It looked like it should be advertising shampoo.

My hair was shorter than his because it turns bushy if I let it get longer than a pixie cut. From overhearing him talking to his friends, I knew he didn't care for it, that he preferred hair like Jean's long locks. Preferred blondes to brunettes like me too. Not that I made a habit out of eavesdropping on him or anything.

He held his hands out, fists closed. I tapped the left one,

9

which turned out to hold a white pawn and gave me first move. He answered my opening with a mirror move and cleared his throat. "So, I heard you won today."

My fingers paused on the pawn I was about to move. Lucas made it clear the first day I met him that he was in Camp Curling-Is-Lame. He couldn't have cared to hear about me and the girls winning. Did he mention it just to throw me off? "Yeah, we did."

"Congratulations."

I moved the pawn. "Thanks."

We made it two more moves before he tried talking again. "Carol says you two are destined to battle for the house title."

"Maybe." It suddenly made sense for him to mention curling. Carol, Adam's sister, played at my club. And every other guy at our school had a thing for her, so of course Lucas would too. She was every bit as attractive as her brother and she worked it like crazy. No boy ever dissed curling to her face. No, with Carol they all acted like it was the most interesting thing ever.

He captured one of my knights. "You don't think they'll make it to the final round or you don't think you will?"

Carol's rink, or Team Nemesis as I called them, and mine were unarguably the two strongest Juniors teams in our club. That might have made us rivals even without her skip, Ellen, being a stuck-up bitch. For the last two years, Ellen and Co had snagged our club's spot in the regional playdowns by winning the annual Catscratch Bonspiel. That they'd yet to make Nationals didn't make me feel any better about it. That we'd taken the Saturday Juniors title from them last year helped a little. Just not much.

"If you're digging for info on Carol," I told Lucas, "you'd be better off hitting up her brother. I don't know her that well."

He looked up from the board with a furrow forming between his eyebrows. His eyes were a deep brown, almost the color of the polished wood of the bar. "You'd have a point if that's what I was doing."

My throat was tight as I swallowed. Lucas's frown gave him

10

a dark, brooding sort of air. Very vampire romance hero. Good thing I was a werewolf girl.

I took a breath and concentrated on the game. After a few moments, he made another move and I followed it quickly. We went on playing in silence and for a while we seemed well matched. Then he started making mistakes. The balance shifted in a few moves, until I was finally willing to look at him again from curiosity.

His eyes weren't on the board. They were focused over my shoulder somewhere.

I twisted to follow his gaze and found Jean leaning against a wall, Adam bending over her with one arm propped near her shoulder. They were nearly touching, their gazes locked on each other and the air between them crackling with electricity.

"Guess that's going well," I said.

"What?" Lucas asked. He waved a hand in the air. "I couldn't hear you over the music."

He was totally lying, but I shrugged it off. "Nothing important. Is the music distracting you?"

"What?" He looked at the game situation and smiled sheepishly. "Yeah, I guess. It's not really conducive to thought."

Not conducive to thought. Who talks like that? Other than Lucas, I mean. "I don't think you're supposed to think to it."

His mouth curved a little on one side. "You want to dance to it?"

"You're not getting out of this that easy." I took his queen off the board with a thunk as his eyes flickered back toward Jean and Adam.

He chuckled despite the loss, but frowned when he noticed exactly how bad his position was. Guess he hadn't been paying attention at all. His fingers tapped next to the board as he tried to come up with a way out of his predicament, but he kept getting distracted by the view across the room.

"You can surrender and free yourself up to stare at them."

His fingers went still. "I'm not staring at them."

"No, but you keep looking over there. Might as well save yourself the eye motions."

11

He shook his head as he made himself look at the game. He moved a bishop, right into the path of my remaining rook. The move was stupid enough that I wasted several moments trying to spot the trap before taking the clergyman.

If Lucas were better at acting, I'd have thought he was trying to throw the game, but I didn't credit him with the skills to fake the level of disgust on his face. He made a halfway decent move with a knight, but followed it up by sacrificing his second bishop to capture a pawn.

"Seriously, dude. Just go over there." Beating him would have fun if he'd been paying attention, but I couldn't find joy in slaughtering an opponent who wasn't even looking at me.

"Aren't you supposed to be keeping me from going over there?"

Oh, right. I'd kind of forgotten that. "Was it that obvious?"

He shrugged. "She dragged him off pretty fast. Plus, you never initiate conversations with me. So, yeah, it was."

I never initiated conversations with him? Well, no. Because when we did speak to each other, it wound up going like this. "You never talk to me either," I muttered.

"Any reason I should?" He'd stopped watching Jean to look at me, his mouth pulling into a sullen frown.

My queen slid diagonally to capture the pawn protecting his king. "Check."

"Check," he repeated, sounding annoyed. Lucas wasn't used to losing at anything other than hockey and I guessed he didn't know how to do it with grace. He moved his king out of check, but it was useless. One more move for my rook and it was checkmate. His fingers flicked the king over and he stood up, leaving the piece dead on the battlefield. "Good game."

"Yeah, good game." It wasn't, not even close, but it wasn't in me to rub that in. I stood up. "I'm going to the bathroom."

Lucas had vanished when I got back, leaving the board exactly like it was. Grrr. I hated people who left things out like that. It's not like it takes long to make things neat. I went ahead and set it back up, quickly before someone could trap me into playing again. If anyone else at the party was lame enough to do that.

I went a bit too quickly. A few pieces fell behind the bar and I had to walk around to grab them. I had them in my hands and was about ready to stand up when two voices came in over the music. Lucas and Adam.

"I'm just saying you need to stop and think." That was Lucas, I'd have known the smarmy overtone anywhere.

"What's your deal, bro? You jealous? You want her?"

The music faded in time for me to get the tail end of a moan of denial. "Don't be ridiculous."

Right. Because it would be ridiculous for him to be into someone like Jean, someone with more brains than boobs, a girl more likely to cure cancer than become a supermodel. Not when he could be lusting after Carol. Though even she was too smart for him.

The music kicked in sudden and loud, drowning out Adam's response though I crawled closer trying to hear it. Something banged against the the top of the bar, like someone had walked into it.

"You okay?" Adam asked.

"Yeah, fine." Lucas sounded distracted and annoyed, like he had for most of the evening. "But, seriously, you need to take a long look at that girl and make sure this is what you want to do."

In my fists, the chessmen dug into my flesh. I had to loosen my grip from fear I'd break the stupid things.

"Yes, Dad," Adam said. I could almost hear the sarcastic look he must have been wearing.

I closed my eyes and counted to ten. Then twenty. Killing Lucas sounded like a great idea, but doing it in front of a room full of people would be stupid. I got to one hundred and stood up.

Lucas sat on the closest stool, his chin resting on a fist as he looked straight at me. His eyebrows went up, but not as an expression of surprise, more like a taunt. A big old, "Whatcha gonna do now?"

I slammed the game pieces down. "You're an asshole."

13

He leaned back, folding his arms across his chest. "Says the girl I just caught spying on me."

"I wasn't spying on you!" I stormed around the edge of the bar.

He jumped from the stool to come after me. "You weren't? Why were you hiding then?"

"Why do you care?" I shook my head and weaved around some people hovering over the refreshments. "I wasn't hiding. I was cleaning. Not that you'd know what that was."

He bumped into someone, barely glancing at her as he offered an insincere apology and kept after me. "Where are you going?"

"Away from you."

"Darcy, I don't think you understood what you heard."

I spun around, so pissed my muscles shook. "Oh? And what did I misunderstand?"

He opened his mouth to answer, but Carol slunk in next to him and wrapped her arm around his. His lips pressed together as his eyes went to her.

"Never mind," I said. "I don't want to hear it. Stay out of Jean's business."

That time when I rushed off, he didn't follow.

TO-DO THIS WEEKEND

1. Beat Team Brinkley.

2. Study for calculus.

3. Essay on mole imagery in Hamlet. (Moles? WTF?)

4. Pretend to care about Kevin's hockey game.

5. Work on personal essay for Catskill application.

6. Find ways of reminding Jean why she shouldn't destroy both our team and our lives by moving to California.

CATSKILL COLLEGE APPLICATION
PERSONAL ESSAY
OPTION 3: THE MOST IMPORTANT THING IN MY LIFE
IS...

The most important things in my life is curling.

Yep, that's right, I'm being honest with you instead of pretending that my life revolves around studying or volunteer work or scientific research. It doesn't. It revolves around curling. The Catskill Curling Club is my home. My team is my family. It's the people more than the sport that make this activity the most important one in my life.

There are only four players on a curling team, so it's not like sports where you might not know everyone on your team as anything other than a name, number, or position.

There's a chain of command, but each player is expected to have an input on decisions even though final say goes to the leader. That leader is called the skipper, or skip. On my team, that's my best friend, Jean. Jean calls the shots and gives the sweepers, AKA the girls with the brooms, commands on when to sweep to make sure the rock goes along the correct line.

I'm our team vice, or third. I help Jean make calls. I give guidance when she's the one throwing the rock down the ice. I'm like the First Officer to her Captain. It's also my job to say how many points were scored in an end and to see the score goes up on the scoreboard.

Our second, Maria...

Ugh. This isn't what they want. Why am I typing it? Why am I typing this? I must need sleep...

Chapter Three

My brother played hockey. It wasn't something I was particularly proud of, but I went to most of his home games anyway, whenever they didn't conflict with my curling schedule. Because if I didn't, my mom would force me to babysit my twin half-brothers. Between hockey and time spent with six-year-olds, I'd chose hockey any day.

Since I wasn't willing to stay home alone with them, Mom brought the half-monsters to the games with her. They ran along the top row of seats screaming, "Go, Kevin!" even when Kevin was sitting on the bench. They never went to the curling club to yell "Go, Darcy!" for me, but that was just as well. If they were screaming my name, I wouldn't be able to pretend I didn't know them.

I sat as far from my family as I could while still being in my school's official seating area. I wasn't quite willing to claim to be there to support the other team.

Jean found me in the second period, drawing me out of an engrossing level of Angry Birds on my phone. "Hey. Kevin get to play today?"

"Not yet." I slid my phone into my pocket and looked out on the ice. "But if we continue to suck this bad he might."

As a sophomore, Kevin didn't get much play under normal circumstances. We were down by three though, so it was conceivable the coach would get desperate soon.

"Where's Adam?"

I pointed to him. "Penalty box. He's been there most the game."

"Been a bad boy, has he?" she asked, innuendo dripping from her tone.

"Has he?" As I stared at her, she started to blush. "What did I miss last night?"

She let out a breath, completely deflating. "Nothing. Nothing at all. I went to move my car for someone to get out and when I came back, he was all distracted and different. I don't know what happened."

I did. Lucas happened. But I didn't want to tell her what he'd said.

"What happened to you?" she asked.

"Too many people." One too many anyway. "I just needed to get out. Sorry I ditched you without saying anything."

"It's alright." She sighed and looked over to where Adam shifted from side to side, waiting to be released. "I would have told you to go. I thought I was getting somewhere."

"It looked like it last time I saw you." Not last time I saw Adam, of course, but...

A pair of skaters slammed into the glass in front of us. One of them was Colin. Jean shook her head as he rushed off again. "Maybe I should have settled for him. At least he knows I'm alive."

I rolled my eyes. "Colin's friends are less annoying. But, sweetie, Adam knows you exist. He keeps looking over here."

"Really?" She brightened, but then her face fell. "Of course he is, the puck's between us."

"It's not just the puck." I was sure it wasn't, although my words lost some of their impact when the clock hit zero and Adam lurched from the box, going straight for the heart of the action. "He probably got scared he'd freak you out if he came on too strong or something."

"You think?"

I bit the inside of my lip as I nodded. It's not like I enjoy lying or practice it often, so I'm sure I was sending out all sorts of tells right then. But she wanted to believe me, so she did.

18

Adam took control of the puck, sending it over to Lucas, who stared at it like he wasn't sure what it was or what he was supposed to do with it. One of the Hudson players hit him with a wicked hip check and zoomed off with it while Lucas tried to regain his breath. I allowed myself to smile, but not to cheer. There was a fine line between pulling against Lucas and pulling against my team.

"Do you think I should try to talk to him after the game?"

I dragged my attention from Lucas's pain, even though I could have watched him get beat up all day. "I don't know. He might not be in such a good mood after this."

"Maybe he'll want sympathy?"

And maybe his teammates will be around, which means maybe Lucas would be there to remind him not to be into Jean. "He's never struck me as that kind of guy."

"True." She frowned, but then leaped to her feet to cheer as the goal alarm went off.

My eyes snapped back to the ice, where Adam was near the far goal, waving his stick in the air and grinning like a madman. I got up so Jean would hear me tell her, "Or maybe he'll think you're a good luck charm. You showed up and suddenly they score."

She clapped like a little kid at Christmas.

It wasn't to be though. There was no miraculous comeback. There weren't even any other goals. And although Jean went against my advice to wait in the parking lot for Adam to come out, he barely glanced at her before jumping into one of his teammate's cars.

"That's okay," she said, nodding as the car pulled away. "We need to hit the gym anyway."

I sighed. I'd been hoping she'd forget about her New School Year Resolution to have two weight days a week so I could pretend to forget about it too. Weight training's important to curling, more important than my preferred cardio for Jean's position, but I hated being trapped inside unless the building had ice in it. Our community gym kept things at a toasty seventy degrees and it smelled like cleaning products and

19

sweat. Locking ourselves in there was a waste of a perfect autumn day if there ever was one.

To make the torture worse, Carol and her bleached-blond curls clanged into the locker room right after we did. She gave us a smile so wide it had to be fake and plopped her bag down next to our stuff like she thought we were friends. "Oh, my God. Can you believe how awful those refs were? Lakeside was all over Lucas and they never called anything!"

No, they didn't. Because all of it had been legal, not to mention fulfillment of karma.

"I know!" Jean said, sticking up for him because she sticks up for everyone she knows, whether or not they deserve it. "But your brother so much as looked at a guy funny and they tossed him in the penalty box!"

"Seriously." Carol shook her head as she unzipped her bag and took out a slinky tank top that looked more like something to wear to the mall than to work out in. "Adam's going to be such an ass tonight, I'm not sure I should go home."

Jean laughed as she wiggled out of her jeans. "I'm sure he'll get over it."

I concentrated on changing clothes and keeping my mouth shut.

"Maybe," Carol agreed. "Depends on which of the groupies he picks up at Burger Zone, I guess."

"Right." Jean's voice dipped in volume and pitch as she smoothed her t-shirt down over her shorts. The smile she gave Carol came nowhere near her eyes. "Well, I hope it works out for him."

We hit the weights. Hard. And we didn't talk about Adam any more, just sang as loud as we could to the synchronized play lists on our mp3 players.

It took a double-length workout, but eventually Jean moved past what Carol had said to get back into her groove. By the time we showered and changed back into our regular clothes, she was back to her old self. Right up until we ran into Lucas Fitzwilliam on our way out.

He shifted from foot to foot in front of the check-in counter

20

as the lady manning it reminded him the pool closed in half an hour. He nodded at her and promised he'd be quick. "I just need to do a few laps."

"Alright," she said. "Go on then."

He couldn't go on though because Jean stepped in his way and didn't move to the side when he approached. I stopped too, worried about Jean.

"Um..." she said.

Lucas raised his eyebrows at her. "Hey, Jean. What's up?"

His eyes flickered to me, but didn't linger to take in the details of my glower.

Jean took a breath and let out a little giggle. "Um... I just wondered... Is Adam okay? He looked pretty upset."

A breeze came in as someone behind me opened the door. All I had to do was turn and sprint and I could be out of the building, away from this stupid conversation. But I couldn't leave Jean, I had to stand there and share her pain as she bumbled along.

"He's fine," Lucas said, readjusting the bag on his shoulder. His half hour of pool time was ticking away.

"Are you sure?" Jean's eyes were huge, pleading. "Because I thought maybe I should... I don't know, call him or something?"

Lucas let out a long breath, his gaze flitting to me again. "I don't think you need to do that."

"You don't?" she asked, her voice almost a whisper.

He ran a hand through his hair and left it resting on the back of his neck. "I'm sorry, but last time I saw him, he was leaving with some girl I don't know. Christie or Christa or maybe Christine? I... I don't think you need to worry about him."

He gave me another look, just for a second, then dodged around Jean and rushed down the hall to the mens' locker room.

21

REASONS TO HATE LUCAS FITZWILLIAM

1. He thinks curling is lame.

2. He thinks he's awesome for playing hockey, even though he sucks at it.

3. He thinks hockey is superior to curling, even though complete morons like himself are capable of playing hockey.

4. He gets mad when I beat his test scores.

5. He wears way too much flannel.

6. He's under the impression orange is a reasonable color for a flannel shirt.

7. His cologne of choice is disgusting.

8. He's actively trying to break my best friend's heart.

Chapter Four

"Hard!" Jean yelled across the ice. "Hurry! Hard!"

Maria and Lisa hurried, sweeping fast and hard. The rock hit exactly where Jean had wanted it. Too bad she hadn't wanted it in the right spot. It knocked into an opposing rock, removing it, but leaving the other team's second rock sitting right on the button and giving them the point we wanted.

Jean made a face, biting back a curse that would have shaken the rafters if we hadn't been practicing next to the Little Rockers. Shouting bad words near the under-ten set wasn't encouraged by club management.

"Again?" I asked, already moving the rocks back to where they started.

"Again," my skip confirmed, her voice filled with disgust.

"Ugh," Lisa said. Her breathing was heavy from all the sweeping her older sister had her doing and her t-shirt was clingy with sweat. She moved a lose strand of blond hair out of her face and glared at Jean. "Seriously? Again? We've been doing this one shot for like an hour now."

That was an exaggeration. It had been half an hour, tops.

"She may have a point," Maria said before meeting Jean's eyes. But after getting a good look at our skip, she shook her head hard enough that her jet black dreads swayed with the motion, jingling the little bells tied into them. "Fine."

The sweepers trudged back to the hog line to wait for Jean to try the throw yet again. She'd missed an identical shot in

23

our last game and it was obviously driving her nuts that she still hadn't figured out what she should have done.

I looked at my other teammates as Jean thought. Lisa was usually nearly as pale as the ice, but her face had a splotchy redness that spoke of too much exertion. Signs of fatigue were harder to spot on Maria's darker African-American complexion, but she swayed a little as she stood, like she really needed to sit down. "Maybe we should do something else and come back to this later, look at it fresh."

But our skip shook her head, obsessed and determined.

"What do you want?" I asked. My job right then was to give her a place to aim, but I couldn't do that if I didn't know what she was trying for. I don't think she heard me over the little kids squealing about their games, but she knew what I meant. She held up a hand and pointed until she had me where she wanted me. We'd already tried this approach, but I went and placed my broom where she ordered anyway. Maybe she planned on trying a different weight than last time. Or maybe she figured the ice had changed enough that it would work now.

One of the things making this exercise frustrating to everyone other than Jean was that ice isn't the same from game to game, or even from end to end. The practice surface wasn't the same surface we'd had the day before. I pointed that out at the beginning, then let it drop. Arguing with the skip isn't something I believe in, especially when it's Jean. When she's obsessed with something, she's as stubborn as the rocks themselves.

The second the shot left Jean's hand, I knew this latest rock wasn't going to do any better than the ones before it. Maria put her heart into sweeping for it anyway, even though we all knew the cause was lost, but Lisa stopped trying about half way down.

Jean started walking up the sheet before the throw made it to the house. She stood and stared as Maria and I got the rocks back in place. "What should I be doing?"

"I think it's the angle," I said. I tapped the target rock with my broom. "You keep hitting between here and here. You need to be hitting here."

"How am I supposed to do that?" she asked. She looked at the guard keeping her from approaching that route. In theory it could be hit into the house, but there was another guard almost on top of it.

Lisa yawned. "Not all shots are makeable, you know."

Jean and I looked at each other.

"This one's doable," said an entirely new voice.

We all jumped just a little. None of us had noticed Hunter Saint George strutting over from the Little Rocks group he helped out with to study our layout. He grinned at the reaction. If Hunter were an animated character, there would have been a burst of light shining out of his dark blue eyes. And if we were cartoons, you could have seen our hearts trying to leap out of our chests in response. Even Maria's, and she doesn't even like boys that way.

Jean got over the shock and Hunter's gorgeousness first. "How?"

"I'll show you."

Full of confidence, he zipped down the sheet to the hack and lined up. He was lithe as he bent and his balance didn't waver at all. He could have been an illustration of the perfect curler.

"What's he doing?" I asked Lisa.

"I think he's going to hit both the guards."

It could work. If you could throw with more strength than any of my teammates, which Hunter most certainly could. I wasn't sure about the angles involved, but I shrugged and got myself out of the way of the shot.

He didn't put as much weight on the rock as I'd predicted and he didn't call the sweepers in until after I expected, but the rock slammed into the first guard just right. First guard hit the second. The second one flew across the ice to smack into the rock Lisa kept hitting at exactly the angle I'd said she needed to find. That rock hit the one sitting on the button. And just like that he'd gotten both of the opponent rocks out of the house, leaving three of ours in scoring position.

"I could have done that," Lisa said. I wasn't sure, but I let her go ahead and think it anyway.

Hunter slid down the sheet with a cocky grin. "What do you think? Am I a genius?"

Lisa giggled, Maria rolled her eyes, and I went completely still. He was looking straight at me. My mouth was suddenly dry and I couldn't quite remember how to speak, so I just smiled at him. I knew I looked like an idiot, but he didn't seem to mind.

"Thanks," Jean said.

"Yeah, thanks!" Lisa virtually leaped in his path, forcing his eyes to her. "We're going to clean up and grab a pizza. Want to come? Our treat, for the coaching."

Coaching? Was that what it was? He'd jumped in and solved the problem, but that's different from teaching us how to deal with it. But any antagonism I felt died a quick death as he looked at me before answering. There was a question in his gaze, like his reply depended on my response. I nodded.

"Sure." He beamed at me, but Lisa was the one who beamed back at him. I was too stunned to do anything beyond just kind of stare.

Petre's Pizza was across the street from the club and was the place for teen curlers to hang. We had a kitchen in the club and the over-twenty-ones tended to socialize there, enjoying the small bar and bringing their own food, but the kids all went to Petre's after we played. They offered discounts to curlers and their décor featured a curling theme. There aren't many places like it south of Canada, but it was founded by a founding member of our club, a guy who's great-grandfather had founded the entire town.

We walked in past the row of pinball machines, greeted by happy beeps, flashing lights, and the familiar aroma of cheese and that concentrated syrup they make pop out of.

Maria's girlfriend, Cat, sat near the pool table. Like after most practice sessions, the cute Irish redhead and her assortment of freckles waited for us with a pitcher of pop and an order of bread sticks at a table painted to look like a curling sheet. An open text book lay in front of her, something with a lot of small writing and equations. Maria and Cat went to the town's only private high school, which was very heavy on advanced academics. Even if my family could have afforded to send me there, I'd never have passed the entrance exam. I was decent at math, but the kids at Maria and Cat's school were scary good, and my English scores just wouldn't cut it. Both girls were a year behind me, age and grade-wise, but were doing work I probably wouldn't get to even in college.

I grabbed one of the places next to our number one fan and the yummy bread sticks she'd so thoughtfully ordered. Early in their relationship, I'd teased Maria that if they broke up, I was keeping Cat. I'd only been half joking.

As Maria leaned over to kiss Cat's cheek in greeting, Hunter stopped walking. He took a second to process the exchange before sweeping into the seat at the end of the table, the one right next to me. I couldn't tell if the gay thing threw him or if it was the interracial thing, neither of which were too common in Meryton, but he recovered quickly and smiled at Cat. "Hey. I'm Hunter."

"Yeah, Saint George. I've seen you curl." She closed her textbook and returned his smile. "You're pretty good."

He shrugged and leaned back in the seat while the rest of us sat down. "Thanks. I was vice of the rink the US sent to Worlds last year."

That tidbit wasn't exactly a secret. Our club was small, and everyone had known before the season even started that our newest junior player had a history including placing second in the World Championship. Most people weren't quite as impressed by it as Hunter seemed to be though.

The arrival of Sherry, who'd been a server at Petre's since before I had teeth, distracted me from deciding if Hunter was being arrogant or just factual in his statement. Cat had already ordered our usual veggie combo, but with Hunter at the table we needed to decide on something else to have as well. And we needed to decide quickly, because at least one of us was starving.

After Sherry left, Lisa turned her eyes to Hunter, giving them a little bat. "So why did you decide to go to school here, instead of staying closer to home?"

He laughed and dunked a bread stick into the bowl of marinara. "Because closer to home means closer to my parents."

"Catskill's also further from your friends," I pointed out. "And you had to leave your team."

He swallowed the huge bite of bread he'd been chewing on. "Team broke up anyway. The skipper's too old now and everyone else wanted to leave town as much as I did. Besides, I have a new team now. One I get to skip."

"Uh huh." I took a sip of pop to hide the frown I felt forming. For me, teams weren't things to change whenever you felt like it. Teams were families. They meant something.

No sooner had I thought about family before a member of my biological one strolled in. There's someone I wouldn't have minded moving across the country.

Kevin walked straight up to us, of course. He pulled out the seat between Lisa and Jean like someone had invited him. He sported a serious case of helmet hair and the scent of spray-on deodorant didn't quite mask the fact that he'd been working out. Clearly, Mom and I had completely failed at teaching him when to shower.

The first of our pizzas arrived and Kev snatched a piece before Sherry even had the dish onto the table. She laughed at him. "Someone's hungry."

I frowned at my brother as he shoved food into his face. "Someone should get his own food. At his own place. Why are you even here?"

He mumbled something that years of practice let me interpret as, "Burger Land's closed. Kitchen fire. Team's coming here."

"What?" Lisa asked. Which was a mistake because he turned to her and repeated the info, his mouth still crammed full of pizza.

28

The bell over the door tinkled as a few other hockey players drifted in. They glanced at Kevin but found their own table. Thank God.

Kev swallowed and grabbed my glass, downing most it in one gulp. Then he finally deigned to notice Hunter, who watched him with faint amusement. "Who are you?"

Hunter's lips turned up and he looked at me. "This is your brother, right?"

Miserable, I nodded.

"Good."

Good? My eyes snapped up to stare at Hunter. The only way it could be good was if he'd been worried I had bad enough taste to be dating Kevin, right? Because it had to be obvious that we were family. But hopefully it wasn't too obvious because I didn't want to look, or smell, like him.

Lisa ignored the word and made introductions. "This is Hunter Saint George. He goes to Catskill and his team's going to be at Regionals with us."

Hunter smiled, his eyes locked on mine. "I hope so."

"Whatever." Kevin stood up as Sherry dropped the second pie off. He grabbed a slice of the new one before abandoning us to his friends.

Lisa shook her head as he left. "Rude much?"

I reached for my first slice. "At least you don't have to live with him."

"Don't be so rough on the kid," Hunter said, his eyes trailing across the room to where Kevin had moved to. "He cares enough about his big sister to check out who she's hanging with."

"He wasn't checking you out," I countered. "He was getting free pizza."

Maria made a thoughtful sound. "Yeah, gotta back Darcy up on that."

"Oh, I don't know," Cat said slowly, a mischievous glint in her eyes. "He did a lot of checking me out to make sure I was a good influence."

Everyone laughed at the memory of Kevin trailing us

whenever Cat was around until it sank into his head that whatever she and Maria may do in private, they weren't going to do anything x-rated while he was around. Jean alone was silent. My appetite sank when I saw her expression. The longing on her face as she watched the door could only be the result of one person.

Just outside the pizzeria, Adam and Lucas stood on the sidewalk talking. Lucas kept shaking his head while Adam waved his hands around. I forced my attention down to my pizza, feeling conflicted. I really wanted Jean to hook up with someone to increase the odds of her staying here next year, but did it have to be Adam? Not only was his best friend an ass, but he listened to that ass. Also, well, Lucas wouldn't have been able to taunt Jean about Christa or Christie or Christine if hadn't been plausible that Adam was off scoring with some random girl. Maybe I should be selling Jean on someone who was less of a womanizer.

I kept my eyes down when the door jangled, but looked up when someone cleared his throat at the edge of our table.

Adam gave us all a weak smile.

Lisa raised her eyebrows at him. "Can we help you?"

"Um..."

"Hey, Adam," I said. "Hungry?"

He glanced back at the door, but Lucas had vanished. Apparently he'd decided he couldn't control his friend and didn't want to witness Adam making as huge a dating blunder as going after Jean. Suddenly, I wanted the two together just to annoy Lucas. Adam may have been a serial dater, but he never cheated on any of those girls, or even dumped them in nasty ways. Jean would be fine with him.

I kicked out my foot and sent the chair next to Jean jumping back a few inches. "Sit down."

For a second, he didn't move. Then Jean smiled and he was in the seat in a flash. Maybe there was hope for them. Maybe.

A movement caught my eye and I turned my head to see Lucas watching from near Kevin, a deep scowl on his face.

AWESOME THINGS ABOUT HUNTER

1. He's a great curler.
2. He's really cute.
3. He's smart.
4. He's enthusiastic about things.
5. He likes my friends.
6. My friends like him.

NOT-AWESOME THINGS ABOUT HUNTER

1. He's a little too aware he's a great curler.
2. He's also aware he's hot.
3. He may not be as smart as he thinks he is.
4. He's a little flashy in his enthusiasm. Not the best of sports.
5. He may like my friends a bit too much...
6. Lisa may like him too much. (Though, to be honest, being Lisa, she'll likely move on to someone else in a week or two anyway. Plus, Hunter's nineteen. That's only a year and a half older than me, but it's four years older than Lisa, so her mom probably wouldn't let them go out anyway.)

TO: darcybennet@merytonhs.com
FROM: jeansmith@merytonhs.com
SUBJECT: Good Hunting?

What in the world was up with you and Hunter today? The boy can't keep his eyes off you! I thought Lisa was going to go freakazoid!

So... You are interested in him, right? I mean, he's really cute and obviously an amazing curler. Not that he's as cute as Adam, of course... :)

Speaking of... You'd tell me if I was making a complete fool of myself, right? Right? RIGHT?

Agh. I've clearly lost my mind. Time to go to sleep.

Love ya, babe.

-Jean

Chapter Five

My stone clicked into the shot rock at just the right angle to nudge it out of contention. Yes! Jean beamed at me from the far side of the sheet and the opposing vice gave me a nod of respect before settling into throwing position herself. It would be a challenge for her to move my rock without knocking hers out of the house too, and her team needed to score with all of their remaining stones.

For a few moments, I thought she managed to pull it off and I started pondering my next shot. But her rock stopped curling before it should have and instead of sending my stone off to the side it sent her team's flying back toward the board.

I groaned in sympathy. "That was close, Manda."

"Story of my season." She shook her head and shrugged an apology toward her skip, a girl named Brandi, who held her hand out to Jean in concession. With only two rocks left to throw and just one in the house, it was physically impossible for Brandi and Manda's team to score the four points they needed to tie, so conceding was polite.

"Season's not over," I pointed out, shaking her hand.

"No." She took my hand with a firm grip, showing no shame in her defeat. "But we're officially playing for third now. You and Boroughs have the top two wrapped up."

I moved on to shake hands with Manda's lead, but still addressed my fellow vice. "We're not even halfway through the season. Nothing's settled."

"Sure it's not. You could all be abducted by aliens." Manda smiled and went on to talk to Jean as I shook with her skip before starting to move our rocks to the side of the sheet.

I wished people would stop saying things like that, even if they were true. There was already talk amongst the adults of not allowing competitive teams to curl in the junior's league, in an attempt to even the odds some. I could see their point, but at the same time I would hate to lose the closeness that playing together all season brings a team. It's just not the same when you're only together for bonspiels. Not that it would matter as much if Jean abandoned me anyway...

Up the ice, I caught a glimpse of Hunter doing a funny little shuffle that made me laugh despite the dark thoughts I'd had a second before. I looked away quickly though, unwilling to encourage him or to be caught looking. Triumphant dances aren't really the kind of thing that flies in curling, a sport that's proud of how polite and civilized it is. Or, well, okay, we're not always that polite. But we're usually not that flamboyant about it. Still, my eyes slid from the rocks I was collecting and back to Hunter.

He watched his opponent's throw with calm detachment. His mouth twitched a little when the other guys' rock didn't go where they wanted it, but he didn't cheer or do anything obnoxious.

Our eyes met across the room and I suddenly felt cold. I'd been standing on ice for two hours, perfectly warm until that instant. It was a good cold though, a delicious and thrilling cold. I wanted to wrap it around me, sink into it until I drowned.

Jean slid into my line of sight, oblivious to what she had interrupted. "You want to hang here or at Petre's?"

I shook off the residue of my Hunter-induced chill and shrugged. "Their choice."

On my way off the ice, I looked over at Hunter again. He was calling a shot for his lead, but he saw me and smiled.

My fingers tingled as I waved and mouthed, "Good luck."

"What was that?" Maria whispered to me as we slipped

34

through the door between the ice and the heated entryway. She smiled at Cat, who trotted down the stairs toward us, but kept her attention on me.

I shrugged. "Nothing."

"Nothing?"

"Well... Mostly nothing. Maybe."

"Mostly nothing, maybe." She shook her head, her dreads swinging in their ponytail. "Well, don't let Lisa catch on then."

I tried not to wince at the reminder of our youngest teammate. Lisa had been distracted all game. While we were playing, I'd ignored it, but now the game had ended, I realized she'd spent an awful lot of time looking in the general direction of Team Saint George. It was too much to hope for that she hadn't been checking Hunter out.

The sun's position near the horizon said it was around four as we crossed the road to Petre's, but the place was more crowded than I'd ever seen it outside of the dinner rush. Brandi wrinkled her nose, making her look less like a Swedish model and more like a pug dog. "Hockey players? Why are there hockey players here?"

"Fire at Burgerland," Jean summarized, her eyes scanning the room for one particular hockey player. Adam was there, but he was surrounded by teammates and though he smiled Jean's way, he didn't extract himself from his friends.

Half-way through a pitcher of pop and plate of fried mozzarella sticks, Hunter appeared and wedged a chair between me and Jean. "Can I sit here? This place is packed."

The table suddenly got a lot more crowded as Hunter's team and their opponents started sliding chairs gathered from the rest of the restaurant up to our table. Hunter had put his chair so close to mine that he climbed over the back of it rather than trying to sit down in a normal way and the second his leg brushed against mine I started feeling lightheaded in a pleasant sort of way. It completely erased the hint of annoyance I felt over him just assuming we wanted eight extra people to join us.

The lightheadedness spiralled into dizzy when he leaned

into me, his breath warming my cheek even as the thrilling cold from the rink came back and sent tingles across the rest of my body. His voice was just loud enough to carry over the background din. "You missed me being brilliant."

My heart raced as I pulled myself together enough to smile at him. "I'm sure you'll do it again sometime."

He grinned and I held back a shiver. "I will."

Lisa scowled at me for a second, but smiled sweetly the instant Hunter looked her way. "So who won?"

Ben, Hunter's rival skip and Cat's next-door neighbor, laughed. "I was just glad to hang on for a full eight ends."

Hunter shrugged, leaving his vice to voice the obligatory, "We got a lot of lucky shots."

The tightening of Hunter's lips told me he didn't agree, but he kept his mouth shut. Which was good, because I didn't want to be between Hunter and Cat if he said anything insulting about her friend.

A few minutes later, a huge chunk of the hockey crowd left en masse, probably on their way to somewhere minors could obtain beer, and my group spread out to take over more tables. Hunter stayed next to me and would have stayed just as close as he'd been if I hadn't scooted my chair over a couple of inches. My hope had been that the added space would get me thinking straight again. It didn't. Awareness of him still swamped my mind, even now that the aroma of pizza and grease had overtaken his scent and every little shift of position didn't leave me rubbing against him.

As we nibbled on fried goodies, I stayed mostly silent and let Lisa take center stage with a diatribe about the opinions of her fellow World History students. She revelled in the attention, not realizing how incredibly young she sounded.

Someone suggested ordering some real food and Hunter raised his eyebrows at me. "You in?"

"Sure."

Jean stood up. "Me too. Gotta run to the bathroom though."

Her look begged me for company, so I did the girly thing and got up too. I didn't make it all the way to the bathroom though. About halfway there, my brother magically appeared in my way and scooped me into a massive hug. "Three assists today, sis!"

Dutifully, I hugged back. "Way to go. You guys win?"

"Nah. We sucked too hard."

"Especially whoever you went in for?"

He grinned and shook his head as he released me. "Lucas just had an off day."

As far as I could tell, he meant it. Even though Lucas on a good day was horrible compared to Kev. It was a travesty that Lucas got to start just because he was the senior.

Jean drew a breath, straightening her shoulders and nodding more to herself than to us. "And Adam?"

"Who do you think I assisted for?" Kevin beamed at her. "He's on fire this year."

"Good." She fell short of sounding earnest, I assumed not because she wanted Adam to fail but because she'd liked the idea of being his good luck charm. Him playing well without her severely dented that idea. "Um... See you around."

My brother frowned as Jean ran off way too fast to look cool doing it. "She must really need to pee."

"Yeah." I nodded, hoping I wasn't giving off a lying tell. I would have said I did too and gone after her, but something in the way Kevin's foot twitched against the floor kept me back. Most people wouldn't have seen that something wasn't just bothering him but bothering the hell out of him, but I wasn't most people. I was his sister. "What's up?"

He shook his head. "Nothing with me. Who's that guy you're with? George something?"

"Hunter Saint George."

He snorted. "Yeah, that's not a pretentious name or anything."

I smacked his arm. "We can't all be named Kevin."

"Yeah." He ran a thumb along his chin, a mannerism he'd picked up from our father. It made more sense on Dad, though. He had a beard. "You..."

I laughed at how uncomfortable he looked. "What, worried

37

about my virtue?"

"No." His face contorted in a sneer, but the ugly look fell when he looked over to the table. It was like a drug had suddenly taken affect on his system, slackening his jaw and making his eyes all droopy. "I was just curious."

Taking pity on him, I didn't mention Lisa's crush on Hunter. "We're not together. But there's definite possibility."

"Yeah?"

Damn, he was looking at me like I'd promised him a car for Christmas. Did he honestly think that if Lisa couldn't snare Hunter, she'd want him? Not being a complete bitch, I kept myself from asking and stuck to nodding.

"You should..." He shuffled some more. "Invite him to the Winter Waltz."

I stared. On what planet would someone in college want to go to a lame high school dance? I felt above it and I was still in high school.

I was so busy staring at my brother, I didn't even notice Lucas coming close until he spoke. "You sound like a girl, Bennet."

The statement was completely accurate, but that didn't give him the right to pick on Kev. I glared for all I was worth. "Excuse me, private conversation!"

Lucas looked around the room. It wasn't packed like earlier, but it wasn't exactly intimate either. "Sorry. I missed the closed door."

"Whatever." I squeezed Kevin's hand and started to walk away. "I'm needed in the ladies' room."

The move only succeeded in ditching Kev. Lucas followed me from the main room and down the hallway to the bathroom. Just before the door, I stopped, worried he might keep after me because the only other door left was the emergency exit. "Ladies' room, dude. You qualify?"

He ignored the question. "Are you going out with Hunter?"

"How is that any of your business?" The yellow lights of the hall reflected off his contacts, distracting me and masking any emotions that were in them. Or maybe there weren't any

38

emotions to hide. There weren't any hints of feeling on the rest of his face.

"Is that a yes?"

I grit my teeth and took a long breath. "That's a why do you care?"

His mouth opened, then snapped shut. He spent a second glaring at me before saying, "I don't. Never mind."

"Now who sounds like a girl?"

His cheek twitched with aggravation and we stood there staring at each other until it seemed beyond ridiculous.

"Darcy..." he said at long, long last. He didn't seem to have any idea what to follow that up with though and shook his head with a frown.

"Lucas..." I edged closer to the door. "Can I go now?"

His eyes dropped to the ground. "I guess."

"Nice talking to you," I said as my back hit the door. "Let's do it again sometime."

"When?"

I stopped opening the door and stared at him. His lips were parted, his eyes wide. He looked like he couldn't believe he'd just asked that. If he could rewind a few seconds, I was pretty sure he would have. Maybe a couple of minutes even.

"Sorry," he said. He shook his head, ran a hand through his hair, and turned to walk down the hall.

"I'll see you at school," I told him.

He stopped to look back over his shoulder at me, but didn't say anything else before I stepped into the bathroom and the door swished closed behind me.

My reflection stared at me from the mirrors over the sinks. I looked completely stunned.

"What happened to you?" Jean asked. She was leaning against the end of the counter, a tube of lip gloss in her hand.

"Nothing." I walked by her into one of the stalls, closing the door quickly so I wouldn't have to see her quizzical expression.

"What did Kevin want?"

"Congratulating."

She laughed, the sound echoing off the tiled floor. "He

39

wanted more than that. What?"

I waited to answer until after I'd flushed. "He wanted to know if I was with Hunter."

"Ah."

"Ah?" Taking my time with my belt only bought me so long. I left the stall to find Jean watching me. "What does ah mean?"

She shrugged. "What makes you think it means anything?"

I turned on the water without comment.

"He wasn't asking about you," Jean said. "He was asking about Lisa."

"How did you know that?" I'd figured out a while back that my brother seriously obsessed over her sister, but I'd never told her about it. It was a little too weird to discuss.

"I'm a genius." She tossed her hair back over her shoulder and gave me a playful smile before turning serious again. "What did you tell him about Hunter?"

"Nothing."

Jean's eyes followed me to the paper towel dispenser. "You keep using that word. I do not think it means what you think it means."

She had a point with her Princess Bride quote. I'd misused the word 'nothing' at least three times that evening. "I told him I wasn't here with Hunter. But that there could be possibilities on that front."

"Oh? Could there now?"

I crumpled the paper towel into a tight wad and tossed it into the garbage. "Maybe. I think. Do you think?"

Her eyes sparkled despite the crappy fluorescent lighting. "I do think."

We grinned at each other and she held out the lip gloss.

WAYS TO HOOK-UP JEAN AND ADAM

1. Lock them in a closet together.

2. Force them on a road trip with each other.

3. Send emails to each, posing as the other.

4. Book them on some kind of dating game show and bribe the host.

5. A rigged game of spin the bottle.

6. Kill Lucas. They can bond over mourning him and he won't be around to keep getting in the way of their bliss.

Chapter Six

Shuffling feet filled the hallways as the school made its reluctant way to the auditorium for an assembly on giving back to the community. Few less enticing reasons to miss class existed and the list of them included things like dental visits and non-elective surgery. But boring as the assembly promised to be, it offered me an opportunity I was determined to use.

Through a mild amount of cleverness, I managed to grab Jean and jump between Lucas and Adam as they went to sit down. I was proud of myself, even though it meant I'd have to spend the entire presentation sitting next to Lucas. No worries, I had a book of crossword puzzles to save me from having to chose between interacting with him and paying attention to the speakers.

I had the book and a pen out before the principal made it to the podium.

"Crosswords in ink?" Lucas whispered as Principal Mather tried to figure out why the mic wasn't working. "Confident."

I shrugged and didn't whisper anything back. I always did crosswords in ink, but not because I was confident. It was more the opposite. When I used pencil I spent too much time erasing answers, debating, and then filling the same word in again.

On stage, Mr. Mather called over backup to help him figure out the mic. You'd think the man had never used the system before.

I filled out one across and two down.

Lucas shifted in his seat. "Hard to believe you went to all the trouble to make sure I sat next to you and now you're going to ignore me."

"I-" My head snapped up and my words froze at his grin. If he wasn't so annoying, it would probably be cute.

He glanced around me to where Jean was whispering something to Adam. "I knew exactly what you were doing."

Feigning indifference, I looked back to my puzzle. "No idea what you're blathering about."

He slid down further in his seat, leaning toward me, getting close enough that I felt his breath against my cheek. For once, he wasn't wearing that awful cologne, but something much more mild. In fact, it may have just been scented soap. It was a massive improvement, but any brownie points it bought him died when he said, "You shouldn't be pushing them together."

"Your opinion has already been noted," I sent back, moving away from him as much as I could without climbing on top of Jean. My pen shook as I filled in three across.

The speakers crackled to life and Mr. Mather made a lame attempt at chuckling. "Alright. Glad we've gotten that all fixed."

I tuned out.

Lucas was silent as the counselor in charge of the volunteerism committee took over. The speech hadn't changed from the first time I heard it three years before, so I didn't feel at all bad about tuning it out.

"Debilitate," Lucas whispered, giving me the answer I was stuck on. The help wasn't appreciated, so I didn't thank him as I scrawled out the answer.

"You should listen," I whispered back. "If you don't get enough hours of mandatory volunteering, you won't get your diploma. Community Service is a graduation requirement."

"Yeah, I read the leaflets." He looked up at the slide on the screen upfront anyway, the one showing the organizations that qualified as school-approved volunteer opportunities. The curling club wasn't on it even though we always needed volunteers for things. Neither was Mom, though I'd argued for years that babysitting for her should count as community service if I didn't charge her anything.

Lucas waited a few minutes, then spoke again. "I don't have anything against Jean."

Wordlessly, I flicked a nasty look his way.

"I don't. It's just..." He twisted, turning more toward me and folding his arms over his chest.

Careful to keep my voice low so it didn't carry to Jean, I turned my head and whispered, "You just don't like her with your friend."

He sighed. "No. No, I don't."

My head shook in disbelief. I couldn't believe he admitted that. "Well, it's none of your business. It's theirs."

His lips pursed into an annoyed moue. His fingers drummed against his arms. He opened his mouth a hair, but turned away without saying anything else.

On my other side, Jean whispered to Adam, completely oblivious to Lucas and his disapproval. What gave him the right to disapprove of Jean? How could he think she wasn't good enough for Adam? Adam was nothing but a stupid hockey player. Sure he was decent on ice, but he wasn't such a great catch. Jean was beautiful. She was funny. She was beyond smart. What the hell was Lucas's problem?

"Fumigate," he said, answering twelve down.

I'd have loved to fumigate him.

Annoyed at the interference, I shifted to make the book harder for my unwanted assistant to see. He shook his head and slumped in his seat, his shoulders now slinking below the top of the chair. If he slid down any further, he'd be in the floor.

"Look," he said after several minutes, "Darcy..."

My grunt of disgust was instant. "Look, Lucas, no one likes to be addressed like that."

He paused for a second. "Sorry. I have undeveloped social skills."

Finally! Something we agreed on!

"I was just going to say..." He took a long breath, during which I filled in nineteen down. "I'll back off if you do."

44

"Hmm?" I looked at him, wondering what he meant.

His chin jerked toward Jean and Adam. "I'll stop interfering if you stop pushing them together."

"Let them work it out themselves, you mean?"

He nodded.

I chewed on the tip of my pen as I considered the offer then plopped it out to ask, "Why do you care, anyway?"

For a while, I didn't think he'd answer. "She deserves better."

My eyes popped open. I'd never heard anyone actually say something like that before, not in real life. "Better like who?"

He shrugged. "Do we have a deal or not?"

There was a smattering of polite applause as someone from the local soup kitchen was announced, but I didn't look at the podium to see who it was because I was staring at Lucas. His eyebrows rose in challenge.

"Yeah, alright." I held my hand out to shake his, feeling like I was sealing a pact with the devil.

REASONS LUCAS MAY HAVE OFFERED HIS NONINTERFERENCE TREATY

1. To trick me into doing nothing while his offensive continues.
2. To mess with my mind and distract me.

WHY?

1. Because he's scared I'm going to win.

WHY DOES HE CARE?

1. Because he hates me.
2. Because he hates Jean.
3. Because he's in love with Jean and wants her for himself.
4. Because he's in love with Adam and wants him for himself.
5. Because he's an ass.

Chapter Seven

If you didn't know anything about Herschel, you'd peg him as a complete wannabe. He's a scrawny Jewish accountant in thick glasses, a cowboy hat, and the kind of clothes you see in country music videos. But those big belt buckles he owns? He didn't buy those at a western wear outlet. Nope, he won those babies fair and square.

I thought Mom was joking when she first mentioned dating a rodeo rider. Mom's more the classic metal and hockey type. In fact, my dad was a hockey player. Left us the second he got called up to the NHL, then washed out in his rookie season and acted shocked Mom wouldn't take him back.

Shel took us out to dinner once a week, a family togetherness project he'd implemented well before he was technically family. At first, I hadn't known what to think about it. On one hand, it seemed kind of presumptuous. On the other hand, he was the first guy Mom had gone out with who viewed me and Kevin as anything other than cock-blocking nuisances.

The twins bounced along the bench seat and I had the honor of being the one to trap them in this week. I glared at Elijah as he ricocheted off my shoulder. They were way too old for this crap.

"Boys!" Mom snapped, sounding exhausted. She thrust a box of crayons at them and a pair of coloring books. "Settle down right now, or you're not getting ice cream."

The customary threat worked like a charm. In an instant,

they went from vibrating balls of hyperactivity to models of good behavior and I was left to read my menu unmolested.

"Hey, Darcy."

I froze at the sound of Hunter's voice and frowned at the list of sandwiches in front of me as I tried to remember what my hair looked like. Had I put on makeup? Was my shirt still clean even though Daniel sat next to me in the van? And, most importantly, why the heck was Hunter at the Grub Barn?

"Hey, Hunter," I said, stuttering a little on his name as I caught sight of his horrid brown Grub Barn t-shirt. It had a chorus line of farm animals on it, which was a little disturbing if you asked me. "You work here?"

"No," Kevin said, rolling his eyes like a brat. "He just digs the logo so much he bought a shirt."

Hunter shrugged. "It was the cow that got me. He's just too cute."

Mom smiled at him, a little too wide. Like she'd forgotten she was sitting next to her husband and didn't realize she was twice Hunter's age. "He's adorable."

The half-monsters started mooing and I froze again, wishing I'd wake up and find out this was a nightmare. But Hunter didn't act like he thought the boys where the lamest thing ever, he grinned at them like they were funny or something. "Can I get you guys anything to drink?"

He took the orders quickly, his eyes staying on me as he wrote mine down. "I'll be right back."

I watched him walk away. The shirt was awful, but I fully approved of his jeans. They were tight enough to show off his rear, but not tight enough to be obscene.

"He's nice," Mom said. I was completely horrified to realize she was checking out Hunter's butt too. Sure, it was a gorgeous one, but sheesh!

"He curls with me," I said, struggling against an impulse toward matricide. "He went to Junior Nationals with his last rink."

"Why'd he move?" Shel asked. His eyes were on his menu and he didn't seem to notice his wife was ogling our server.

Kevin decided to field that one. "He goes to Catskill. But he's a freshman, so it's perfectly acceptable for him to date Darce. He's only a year older than she is."

Either Mom found this interesting or she couldn't see Hunter anymore anyway, because she started staring at Kev instead. "I don't know..."

Shel frowned at me. "Has he asked you out?"

"No." I shook my head. "And he's not going to after seeing me with you people."

"Probably not," Shel agreed. He looked down again. "Do you think I should get the French Dip or a burger?"

"French Dip's better," I said, thankful for the subject change. "Their burgers are frozen."

"Oh, that's right." He nodded. "Good save."

Kevin wasn't done talking about Hunter though. "I could mention to him that he should ask you out."

I slammed my menu down, making a loud enough sound that a lady two tables away gave me a disapproving glower. "You do anything like that and I'll tell Lisa that you take pictures of her when she's not looking."

"He does what?" Mom asked in alarm.

"That's a lie!" Kevin yelled.

The woman across the way put more energy into glaring at us.

"Kevin." Mom held a hand out. "Phone."

He grumbled and handed it over.

It took her a little while to find his photos and she was still trying to figure out how to erase the ones of Lisa when Hunter popped up again and started putting drinks in front of everyone.

Daniel stood up on the seat and pointed at Hunter. "What's your name? And why won't you date my sister?"

Hunter faltered, nearly spilling my pop as he put the glass down. "Um... My name's Hunter."

"And..." Elijah prompted as I slunk down in my seat and prayed for death.

"And," Shel said, "you two are being very rude. Why don't

49

you tell Hunter what you want to eat instead of embarrassing Darcy?"

I barely managed to get out my request for a grilled chicken salad, and excused myself to go to the bathroom as soon as Hunter left. I knew that if I stayed, at least one brother would be beaten senseless.

My phone was out the second the door closed, dialing Jean for some moral support.

She listened, making appropriate noises at the right places and finally concluding, "How horrible! Absolutely mortifying! What did Hunter say after that?"

"Nothing. Except, you know, something about our food being right out." I frowned at my reflection. My hair was waving in all sorts of directions, like drunken porcupine spines. If I'd expected to see anyone I cared about impressing tonight, I'd have have put some product in it.

"What are you going to do now?"

I smoothed down a patch of hair only to watch it spring back up. "What can I do? I'm going to go out there and try to eat dinner without my waiter realizing I'm with the other people at my table."

"Yeah, good luck." She laughed softly. "I'm really sorry. Want me to do something to get back at Kevin?"

"Not yet. Let's take our time and think of something good."

"I'll be working on it," she promised before hanging up.

When I left the room, I nearly jumped out of my skin.

Hunter lounged right across from the door, his arms folded over his chest and his gaze steady on me as I walked out. I couldn't tell if he was angry or just intense. Likewise, I couldn't tell if the situation was creepy or hot.

"Stalk bathrooms often?" I asked.

He pushed off the wall and took a step closer to me. "Just wanted to make sure you were alright. You looked like you might do something drastic."

"Drastic? Me?" I shook my head.

"Hmm." His head tilted to the side as he looked at me. "We good then?"

"Why wouldn't we be?"

His mouth quirked up in the corners, bringing forth the tiniest of dimples. "Always answer questions with questions?"

I started to smile back. "Why would you ask that?"

He laughed. The deep sound sent a pleasant shiver through my body. It stopped too soon. "I've gotta get to the kitchen. But I'll see you at the club Saturday."

It wasn't a question, so I could confirm it. "Yeah. Saturday."

I went back to the table feeling a little less like killing everyone in my family.

WAYS TO GET BACK AT KEVIN

1. Tell Lisa about the pictures. Though it's less effective now that Mom's deleted the proof.

2. Consider us even because I did let Mom know about those. But, really, that's not as bad as what he did. (IE, encourage the half-monsters to humiliate me in front of Hunter.)

3. Make a banner for the half-monsters to wave at the next hockey match proclaiming, "Kevin loves Lisa!"

4. Something involving underwear.

5. Something involving baby pictures.

6. Something involving the school PA system and really bad poetry.

FROM: hstgeorge@catskill.edu
TO: darcybennet@merytonhs.com
SUBJECT: Batman Rulez!

Hey, Darcy! One of your totally awesome little brothers left a really boss Batman at the Barn when you guys left. I'll give it to you Saturday if that's cool.

Unless it's actually Kevin's. From the way you were glaring at him all evening, I assume you want me to keep it if it's his. Maybe blow it up or something?

Peace and Love,

Hunter

Chapter Eight

The second my palm opened up, I knew my throw was too heavy. At the beginning of the game, when the ice was still slow, it might have been alright. But we were in the eighth end and the ice was slick. My shot was going to slide straight through the house. Its only chance at redemption was hitting something.

It came close, brushing past one of the opponents' stones with maybe a millimeter between them, but the aim wasn't bad enough to make the shot good.

Jean gave me a shrug and a little 'it's cool, these things happen' smile. But it wasn't cool, not to me, because that wasn't my first missed shot. We throw two stones per end. That was my fifteenth stone. Maybe three of them had landed near where I wanted.

My sweepers made it back as I lined up in the hack. "Sorry, guys. I don't know what's wrong with my weight today."

"It's okay," Maria said. "We can't be curling goddesses all the time."

She meant it, but the words didn't make me feel any better. I don't ask to be a goddess on ice, just not to be a complete idiot.

I shook my head, muttered, "Thanks," and looked up to study Jean's call. Not that it made that much difference what she asked me to do, I clearly wasn't going to be able to pull it off. And, yes, I was aware negative thoughts are poison. It's just hard to escape them when you're having as bad a game as I was.

I pulled back, lunged forward... The rock slid from my hand... And slid down the ice. Straight as an arrow and without a hint of curl.

The stone clunked into one of our own.

Jean smiled down the ice. "Hey, that's okay too! If you wanted to just freeze it, you should have said so!"

It would have been fine if that was the closing shot. But there were five stones left and I'd just given the other team a chance at a double take-out.

They took it, knocking the only two stones we had in the house out.

It was down to just the skips. The other team was up by one, had last rock, and were laying three. If we pulled out of this, it would be a miracle. Like when Sweden won the Olympic gold in Women's Curling back in 2010 even though Canada looked like they had it in the bag. Just, you know, with a smaller audience and no medal in the offering.

My whole team was there to stare at the layout. Jean took a long breath. "What do you think, girls?"

What I thought was that it was hopeless. We could easily get a rock closer to the button than their stones, but they'd just knock it out next throw.

Lisa shrugged like it was obvious. "Curl in behind them like Darcy was supposed to do."

"Uh-uh," Maria said. "Darcy threw just fine, the ice isn't curling."

"I don't see any other choice," Lisa said, sounding annoyed that Maria hadn't teamed up with her to dis me.

Two sheets down, Hunter was watching us. I looked away fast, dropping my eyes to the ice even though I'd memorized what was there. "Maybe if you throw really wide you can get more curl. I think it's just the center giving us trouble."

Jean grunted. "I like throwing wide. I don't like curling behind."

"Take-out?" I asked, catching on to the plan. It was a hard

55

shot, but she could take out two of their stones. "I kind of like letting them guard us."

We all stared for a few seconds longer.

Finally, Jean nodded. "Alright. I'll try your shot over, but give it twice the ice."

I lined up to give her something to aim at, putting my broom twice as far from where we wanted the stone to end up.

Perfectly still, I waited for Jean to line up and throw.

My teeth dug into my lip as I focused on the rock traveling up the sheet toward me. It was wide. Very wide. It needed to curl back in...

Maria looked up and down quickly, her eyes traveling from the stone to the house. "Weight's light..."

Yeah, it was. That wasn't good. Too light a weight meant it wouldn't travel as far as we needed without sweeping. But if we swept, it wouldn't curl enough.

"On!" I yelled. "Hard!"

Maria and Lisa swept for all they were worth, short rapid attacks on the ice.

"Hard! Hard!"

I ran up, helping give the rock some more weight.

It slammed into the left stone.

I moved fast, sweeping in front of our rock as it moved behind their center.

"You could have called that," I yelled up at Jean.

She laughed, shook her head, and stepped out of the way so the other team could decide their approach.

They went straight down the middle, crashing their laying rock into ours and sending ours shooting out the back of the house.

The situation looked a lot like it had before Jean's first shot, except now there wasn't anything in place to bounce off of. If the shot went wide to the left again, we wouldn't be able to get it to score.

Jean looked for a while, then without asking for opinions told me, "Line up the shot I gave you last time."

Even if she did it better than I had, I wasn't sure that was a great call. It would leave us with a rock in the center, yeah, but they shouldn't have any trouble repeating their last shot and getting rid of it.

Of course, I couldn't think of anything better to suggest.

My broom touched the ice and I held my breath until the rock was out of Jean's hand.

It glided down the sheet.

And then, right where it needed to, it started to curl.

Son of a bitch.

It wasn't the ice. It was me. Part of me had known that already, but denial's so much easier than accepting the fact you suck.

"Weight's good," Maria said.

The weight was perfect. The curl was perfect. The stone swished right to the button.

"Good shot," I called.

"Thanks!" Jean smiled at me as she stepped aside for the other team. There wasn't an ounce of recrimination in it. She'd always been more forgiving than me.

The opposing skip lined up in the hack and all I could do was wait to see if she pulled her shot off or not.

She threw... Straight. Heavy... But maybe not heavy enough.

She hit the rock she meant to, sent it toward ours. But it didn't slam into ours like she'd wanted, it gave it more of a tap...

"Who's got it?" she asked as she and Jean both walked down the sheet.

Their vice and I stood over the center, looking. We were the ones who had to agree which stone was closest to the middle. And it was close. Really close.

But they had it.

I shook my head and tapped their rock. "It's yours. Good game."

"Are you sure?" she asked, squatting down to look closer. "We could measure."

"Nah." I smiled. "I'm sure."

57

Jean came to a stop beside me. "What's the verdict?"

"Their point."

She glanced at the rocks, then nodded and held her hand out to the other skip. "Congratulations. Good game."

Lisa managed to make it past all the hand shaking before she started in on me. "We had shot rock! Why'd you give it to them?"

"Theirs was closer," I said softly.

"You should have measured." She glowered at me like I'd shot her poodle. "I can't believe you! First all those bad shots, then you just give them the game!"

"Lisa," Jean snapped, as close to angry as she ever got. "Shut it!"

Maria looped her arm around mine in a show of solidarity. She leaned to whisper in my ear. "It was their rock. But if I say that louder, she'll just yell more."

I smiled, knowing she was right.

We headed across the way to Petre's. It was still fairly deserted. A few hockey players hung around because their burger place had yet to re-open, but practice had been out for long enough that most of them had gone home. My brother wasn't around, but Lucas and Adam were.

Jean saw Adam a heartbeat after I spotted him. I could tell because she stopped walking for a second and almost caused our opposing lead, Sherilyn, to crash into her back.

Sherry stumbled and glared until she connected Jean's expression with the boys. A forgiving, sympathetic smile replaced her scowl. "Those guys go to your school, right?"

"Yeah," Jean said, snapping back to us, on the move again. She touched a chair at a table near the front, waiting for the rest of us to nod it was alright before pulling it out.

A week ago I would have nudged her toward the corner, to a table near Adam's so I could call him over. But with Lucas looking right at me, I had no choice but to abide by that stupid agreement we made. Even if I had no way of telling if he was living up to his end of it or not.

He kept looking at me as he ate. Did he trust me that little?

I was on the opposite side of the table from Jean, all of both teams between us, but he was staring like he was sure I was about to launch into action. It didn't even stop when I started glaring to let him know I'd noticed the scrutiny.

So I sat there, trying not to look miserable, because then I'd look like a bad sport. I wavered between a desire to break down crying in frustration over just how bad I'd sucked and the burning urge to run across the room and throw a chair at Lucas. If he didn't stop looking at me, I didn't know how long I could fight the temptation.

I was being ridiculous. Over the curling, not over wanting Lucas to look at anything else. Seriously. What did he think I was going to do?

Ugh. Why had I sat where I could see him? I should have sat where Maria was and spared myself the view. Would everyone think it was really weird if I asked to trade spaces? What if I told them it was a game of musical chairs?

I turned in my seat, putting as much of my back to Lucas as I could, and pretended to be really interested in Sherry and Lisa's discussion about some reality show I'd never seen. When the cheese sticks arrived, I stuffed one in my face and wondered exactly how soon I could leave without being rude.

My cheeks were puffed out with mozzarella when a hand fell on the back of my chair. I knew without looking up who was behind me. The only guy Lisa would be preening over the sight of. I tried to chew fast.

"Hey, Darcy," Hunter said smoothly. "My team's heading to the club. But I wanted to give you that toy."

Lisa's voice shot out like a bullet. "Toy?"

I nearly choked at her tone. I struggled to swallow, making myself cough.

Hunter patted my back. "You okay?"

Everyone was stared at me. Except, oddly enough, Lucas. He had a sudden fascination with picking something off his pizza.

"Yeah, I'm fine." I made myself laugh. "Just forgot how to eat for a second."

"Yeah, that can be tricky." Hunter smiled at me and I felt better than I had all day, even though Lisa scowled like I'd run over her favorite sweater with a lawn mower after shooting her poodle.

"So, you have Elijah's Batman?"

"I do." He reached into his coat pocket and brought the action figure out with a flourish.

Our fingers touched as I took the toy and chill bumps sprang up all over my body.

I admit, my voice may have wavered a bit when I said thanks. His fingertips detoured to brush against my wrist and I was a bit distracted.

"No problem."

It wasn't until after he was out the door that I started to breathe again.

"Elijah left it at dinner the other night." I stood the figure on the table beside me. He looked ready to defend me from The Joker. Maybe he could get Lucas to stop watching me? Because he'd gone back to doing that. But he'd also given up on eating and was standing up, so with luck he'd be gone soon.

Lisa made a choking sound. "You had dinner with Hunter?"

"Yeah," I said. "And I took along the half-monsters to test how good a dad he'd make."

The look of alarm on her face was priceless, but I took pity on her. "He works at the Grub Barn. We went there for family night because Kevin loves their pork ribs."

"Aren't you Jewish?" Sherry asked. I could have kissed her for it.

"No," I answered easily. "My step-dad is. So he can't eat the ribs, but Kev and I can have all we want."

"Oh. Yeah, I met him once. I had on one of my club shirts at work and he came in talking about his daughter the curler."

His daughter. Not his step-daughter. It gave me a happy little glow, though I'd have died rather than let on about it.

The conversation moved on without me and my eyes went back to Batman. Batman had been hanging out in Hunter's pocket. Lucky Batman... Plastic probably wouldn't hold scent well, but before I gave it to Elijah I'd check and make sure it didn't smell like Hunter.

I was so engrossed in contemplating Hunter's aroma that I failed to notice Lucas until he was inches away.

"Nice action figure." He picked it up, not bothering to ask if that was alright. "I used to have one like this."

"Yeah. It used to be Kevin's." I held out my hand for it, but he didn't take the hint to give the toy back. Rather, he turned it and gave the back a close look.

"Mine used to have a cape. Think this one did too." He pointed at slots in the back where the cape was supposed to slide in.

I gasped. He was right. Batman did have a cape. He had had one last time I'd seen him anyway. I sprang up and grabbed the figure. "I better see if Hunter's still around. Elijah will throw a fit if he notices."

My chair clattered as I pushed my way around it. It probably would have fallen if Lucas hadn't grabbed its back in time.

I pushed through the door and immediately started shivering. The temperature had plummeted while I was inside, and the air tasted like a freeze was coming soon.

Leaves rolled across the parking lot, carried on a wind that stole what was left of my warmth. They'd all be gone soon. We couldn't be too far away from our first snow.

I stopped when I hit the sidewalk.

I could see across the street, see the cars parked at the club. See Hunter leaning against the hood of his. See the girl between him and the metal, her arms wrapped around his shoulders and her legs wrapped around his waist.

I spun away. And nearly whacked right into Lucas, who was staring across the street with a dazed expression.

I dodged Lucas and kept on going.

Halfway home, I remembered I'd driven. But I didn't go back for my car until morning.

TO: darcybennet@merytonhs.com
FROM: jeansmith@merytonhs.com
SUBJECT: Spill!

So, you went after Hunter... And... WHAT HAPPENED? I saw your car in the lot and his was gone. Where'd he take you? What did you do there? Why won't you answer your phone???

-J

TO: jeanbennett@merytonhs.com
FROM: darcypryce@merytonhs.com
SUBJECT: RE: Spill!

As you know from my text, I'm fine. I'm not with Hunter. I don't know who Hunter's with, but it's not me.

I walked home. Sorry I left without saying goodnight. I... Saw something I didn't want to when I left. See above for a clue.

I'll call you in the morning.

-D

Chapter Nine

When I pulled into my driveway after fetching my beat-up hand-me-down car, I parked next to Jean's two-year-old Mustang. She did a little better in her parents' divorce than I'd done in mine, possibly because her dad got kicked out a month before she got her driver's license.

She sat on her hood as she waited for me and I tried not to draw a parallel between that and Hunter's position last time I saw him. I failed and had to look away before I did something stupid like start crying.

It wasn't like I had a reason to feel this upset. He hadn't betrayed me or anything. Yeah, I'd been getting the impression he was into me. I was wrong. Big deal. It's not like I was in love with the guy. Didn't even have that massive a crush. But no matter how often I reminded myself of that, tears still kept prickling my eyes.

Jean and I watched movies all day while Shel took the step-monsters out, Mom locked herself in her study, and Kevin... I wasn't sure what Kevin was doing, but he wasn't doing it near me so I didn't really care.

By Monday I was fine. Mostly. Maybe a little tired because I couldn't get to sleep wondering who that girl had been, but plenty of people are tired on Mondays.

Lucas moved from his usual seat in government to take the one next to me. He was silent through class, but when the bell rang he stopped me from leaving. "Was your brother okay about the cape?"

I smiled faintly, sure it looked fake. "He never even noticed."

"Ah. Good."

I left before he could ask anything else.

By the time school let out, I was finally ready to fall asleep. I managed to keep myself awake until I got home, then clunked out cold until Mom woke me up for dinner.

"Are you okay, honey?"

"Yeah." I stretched, wanting to roll over and go back to sleep but knowing I had homework to do. "Just sleepy."

She gave me a long look. "Uh huh. Nothing to do with whatever you were pouting about yesterday?'

"Not a thing."

I wiggled past her to the bathroom, shutting the door quickly.

"Brush your hair while you're in there!" she called after me. "We're going to have company over for Monday Night Football. One of them's a boy. I think you know him."

I opened the door to stare at her. "You're kidding. Who?"

"Someone whose dad works with Shel." She smiled mysteriously.

Who's dad worked with Shel? Who's dad... My eyes narrowed. "He's not on Kevin's hockey team, is he?"

Mom's smile got wider, like she couldn't hear the horror in my voice. "He may be..."

With a groan of anguish, I slammed the door. Ugh. That woman could be maddening. Almost as maddening as Lucas Fitzwilliam. Who was apparently coming over to my house for some reason. What reason? Because my parents hated me?

My hair needed more than brushing. I had a serious case of bed-head going on.

Did I care?

No.

Not at all.

But if Lucas's dad came over too... Well, I'd never met him because he'd just started working at the company and I didn't want to embarrass Shel... So I jumped into the shower really fast to get my hair into a manageable state before putting on fresh clothes and heading downstairs.

Mom gave me a knowing smirk when she saw me. It was almost enough to make me turn around and change into the grungiest things I owned.

A crashing sound from the twins' room distracted both of us, getting Mom to sprint up to investigate and leaving me free to roam into the kitchen to see what Shel was up to.

There's a stereotype that men don't cook, but there's also a stereotype that cowboys aren't Jewish. My step-dad wasn't a guy to pay much attention to what people expected of him. It was probably my favorite thing about him. That and his amazing potato skins.

He took a tray of those from the oven as I came in. They sizzled with cheesy goodness and my stomach rumbled with anticipation.

"Was that you?" Shel asked. "Have you eaten today?"

Now that he mentioned it... "Not really."

"Darcy." He gave me an aggrieved look. "We've talked about you skipping lunch."

"Yeah, yeah." I trudged over to the fridge and opened it. The potatoes were too hot to eat and my body didn't want to wait. I was pretty sure I'd eaten the day before, but I'd skipped breakfast as well as lunch.

"Don't yeah yeah me." Shel banged the oven door closed with more force than the task required. "You promised. No skipped meals."

"I know. I'm sorry." It wasn't like I'd fade away to nothing after one day of not eating right, but Shel's niece was hospitalized for anorexia, leaving him a little paranoid about me. But I didn't skip meals because I wanted to be skinny. I skipped them because I got too busy to remember them. Or, occasionally, because the guy who I thought liked me had made out with someone else. "What's the most fattening thing in here?"

"Probably the quiche."

65

Quiche. Not my favorite thing in the world. I knew it would make him feel better if I ate it though, so I grabbed the dish and cut a slice. Heating quiche doesn't make me like it any more, so I went ahead and ate it cold. I was hungry enough for it to taste good.

Not being a complete stranger, Shel had to have known something was up, but he didn't press me about it. Or tease me about getting presentable for our guests, though I was pretty sure he noticed my damp hair.

"When you're done with that," he said, "there's cake."

I'd just finished the smallest slice of German chocolate I could get away with when the doorbell rang. I ignored it, putting my plate in the dishwasher and resisting an urge to check my appearance. I mean, I saw Lucas every day. And I didn't care what he thought about how I looked. Plus, unless I'd gotten cake on my face, I looked the same as I did last time I checked.

Voices approached the kitchen as I picked up a rag and wiped off the counter where I'd eaten. One of them was Shel's. "I have no idea where Kevin's gotten off to, but Darcy's in here."

I tossed the rag into the sink and turned around just as he came into view.

My lips parted at the guy who followed him in. He was tall and my age, did a bad job playing hockey, and even went to my school. But that was all he had in common with Lucas. I should have known there was more than one player on Kevin's team who's dad worked with Shel, but I'd completely forgotten Colin existed. I plastered a smile on my face quick as I could. "Hey, Colin. What's up?"

"Not much. You look nice."

Shel opened the fridge and got drinks for his guests as I contemplated running upstairs and hiding in my room. Where the heck was my brother?

"So..." Colin slunk across the kitchen, stopping just before me. He tried to tilt his head down while smiling up at me. I assumed it was supposed to be a charming look, but it came off a little crazy. "Who are you pulling for?"

"Calculus."

He stopped trying to look charming and looked confused instead. "Calculus?"

"Yeah, I can't watch the game. I have too much homework,"

"Oh." His shoulders slumped for a second but he rallied quickly. "I could help you. I did the assignment already."

My instinct was to say no. I didn't need help, not really. Calculus wasn't nearly as hard as its reputation had made me expect. But, on the other hand, it wasn't much fun for me either. And Colin wasn't that bad. Considering that I could have been talking to Lucas... Who would never have offered to help me with my homework. Not when he gets so pissed every time I beat him on tests.

"Yeah, okay."

But twenty minutes later, I was regretting my decision to open up my textbook on the dining room table. At least I could see the game from where I was, so the evening wasn't a complete snore. But unfortunately, I could also see Colin. Worse, I could hear Colin. By the end of the first quarter, he was one patronizing comment shy of getting punched.

"Thanks for the help," I said, cutting him off in the middle of explaining a simple problem. One which he was getting wrong. "I think I've got it now. And I've just remembered I need to read like fifty pages for English. I don't have calc until after study hall, so..."

"I can do it for you. Then you'll just have to copy it."

Yeah. Copy and correct it. "Thanks, but I wouldn't feel right doing that."

He smiled. "I like your honesty."

"It's a virtue. And a curse." I shrugged. It was also a complete lie. I'd knocked out my English assignment while skipping lunch.

"I like a lot of things about you," he said, his voice dropping low.

Running away screaming would probably be considered rude, but I put serious thought into doing it anyway. "Thanks."

67

He reached out and took my hand. It took a lot of determination not to shudder at the sweat on his palm. I tried to tug my hand back, but he held tight.

In the corner of my eye, I spotted Mom coming down the stairs from tucking the twins in. For a fleeting second I thought I was rescued, but Colin wasn't embarrassed for her to see what he was doing and she, traitorous woman, didn't say anything to make him stop. Nope, she smiled like it made her happy to see her daughter getting pawed. "How are you kids? Can I get you anything?"

Colin smiled back at her. A slick, smarmy smirk of a smile. "No, ma'am."

"I'm going upstairs," I said, freeing my hand with a quick jerk. "I have English. Can't concentrate on football and Tolstoy."

Mom laughed. "How do you concentrate on Tolstoy at all?"

"I'm gifted that way."

Colin tried another shot at charming me. "You're gifted in a lot of ways."

And still Mom didn't kick him out of the house. Too bad Shel was paying too much attention to the Patriots' offense to defend my honor.

I slammed my textbook closed and stood up. "See you at school, Colin."

It looked like I might escape, but Colin snagged my elbow as my foot hit the bottom stair. "Wait up a sec."

Reluctantly, I stopped. As I forced myself to look at Colin, cheers erupted in the sitting room. "You're missing the game."

"I don't mind." He slid his hand down my arm and tried to grab my hand again, but I moved up a step to keep him from succeeding. "Look, I know you have work to do. But I wanted to ask you about something..."

My stomach rolled at his tone. Why had I eaten so much? I edged up another step. "I'm not feeling very well all of a sudden."

"You did go really pale just then." His lips slid up in a thin crescent, like he enjoyed making me nervous. "Is that my

68

fault?"

"No." I put a palm against my stomach as it tried to rebel. "I think I ate something I shouldn't have."

He nodded, but not like he believed me. "So, I was wondering if you'd like to go to the Winter Waltz with me."

Yep, I shouldn't have eaten.

I shoved past Colin, sprinting for the guest bathroom. I barely made it to the toilet before I started to vomit.

TO: darcybennet@merytonhs.com
FROM: jeansmith@merytonhs.com
SUBJECT: What's Wrong?

Hey, babe. What's up? The school says you're sick. Are you? Or did you just say that?

Also... Are you really going to Winter Waltz with Colin? Because he's telling people you are... Maybe that's evidence you really are sick? (Just kidding if you really are going with him. Though not if you aren't...)

And also... Here's your homework assignments. Let me know if you want me to bring any of your books to you tomorrow.

Get well soon...

-J

Chapter Ten

It wasn't Colin's question that set my stomach off, even though it seemed that way at first. It was a stomach flu that most of my family came down with. The next few days weren't much fun.

I dragged myself to school Friday. I still didn't feel great, but if I didn't go Mom might make me skip curling the next day and I was determined not to do that. Although if I was as off my game as I'd been the week before, maybe letting Cat play as a sub would be better for the team... I'd decide after I made it through classes.

Jean inched toward me in homeroom. "I missed you."

"Missed you too." I smiled, wondering if I looked as pale as I felt.

She twisted one of the rings on her right hand. It had a chunk of granite on it and my right hand sported one just like it. We also had team necklaces, little silver penguins, but I was the only one who ever wore mine except on game days. "So... You never answered me about Colin..."

"What about Colin?"

Her fingers went still. "Didn't you get my email?"

I shook my head. "I've been too sick to sit up. Email was the last thing on my mind."

"Oh, crap. I knew I should have texted instead." She drew a slow breath, then leaned closer and said something too quiet for me to hear.

"If it's a secret, you could write it down."

She looked around, like someone in a spy movie worried about the other side tailing them. No one paid attention to us, they were busy with their own conversations. Except Lucas, but he seemed enthralled by something on his laptop. Maybe it was an article for journalism. As one of the senior writers on the paper, most weeks he had some last minute article that someone else had "forgotten" to do to spew out Friday morning for the weekly issue.

"Colin said he asked you to the Winter Waltz."

I groaned. "Well, yeah, he did. Seconds before the virus kicked in."

"The virus kicked in?" Jean asked. "Is that why you said you'd go with him?"

"I didn't say that!" I didn't think... I replayed the memory. Question. Nausea. Vomit. Nope, no answering. "I started puking my guts out."

In front of me, Lucas turned slowly. He had new glasses. They were bronze and brought out little metallic flecks in his eyes. Unlike his old glasses, he looked better in these than in contacts. "Not to butt in, but... He asked you out and you threw up on him?"

"Not on him," I corrected. "Not that it's any of your business, but I made it to the bathroom."

"Still, doesn't sound like a yes to me."

"It wasn't." I folded my arms and leaned back in my seat. "Is this an official interview?"

"No." One corner of his mouth slid up.

"Good. Then get back to whatever you were typing."

That corner of his mouth returned to its usual place. "Glad you're feeling better," he said before turning around and staring at his screen again.

I leaned to the side, trying to see what he was working on for a second before I remembered that I didn't care.

Jean cleared her throat. "Actually, Lucas..."

He turned around again, eyebrows going up.

"Why do you think Colin would do that? Tell people they

were going to the dance if they're not?"

I gave Jean a disgusted squint. "And what, Lucas should know because they're the same gender?"

She shrugged and asked him, "Do you?"

"No." He shook his head. "Unless he figures she'll just go with it rather than contradicting him."

I snorted. "Really? You think he's betting I'd rather go out with him than correct people?"

He shrugged. "Some girls might. Not you, obviously, but..."

"What do you mean by that?" I asked, glaring.

"Um..." His eyes flicked to Jean, begging her for help. "I just meant you're not that easy to manipulate. It wasn't an insult."

"Right. So you didn't mean I'm argumentative?"

Jean started laughing, covering her mouth but failing to stop the sound escaping. "Argumentative? You? No! And you're certainly not someone who'd jump down a guy's throat for saying you're not an idiot."

My mouth froze, partway open with a retort. Then it closed before I turned back to Lucas and gave him a little smile. "Sorry. I may still be a little sick."

"No worries," he said as the bell rang. He grabbed his laptop off his desk and stood up, but paused before leaving. "Let me know if you want a correction in the paper."

I narrowed my eyes at him, but before I could say anything snarky I noticed the way his cheek twitched with the effort to pretend to be serious. "No. But save some space to cover me kicking his ass if he doesn't drop it."

Lucas grinned. "And I hope you win. I've got twenty bucks riding on it."

THINGS TO DO TO COLIN

1. Puke on him.

2. Sue him for defamation of character.

3. Say nothing and let him spend money on a date that's never going to happen.

4. Let Lucas write something about it. He already made a passive aggressive mention in his article on the Winter Waltz. (It ended with a warning to make sure your date had actually agreed to be your date. Ha!)

5. Tell Shel and get him to hogtie the jerk.

6. Go along with it even though that's likely to lead to option one anyway.

Chapter Eleven

Petre's seemed deserted when we walked through the door after a narrow victory, and it took a second to spot what had changed. I'd gotten used to the place having way more testosterone than usual, of the noise and the smell of hockey players. But not a one was there.

Burger Land had finally re-opened, thank God and contractors.

We grabbed a table, rejoicing in having the place back. We even decided to take advantage of the suddenly-open pool table, me and Jean playing Cat and Maria while Lisa tried to climb into Hunter's lap... Well, okay, she wasn't quite that bad, but she couldn't have been more blatant if she'd tried.

As for Hunter... I tried not to look at him. I was so over the guy. Had been for a full week now.

But he looked so good...

Maria made a hissing sound as I watched a shot I'd made. She wasn't commenting on the way the seven ball bounced around the pocket without sinking though, she was looking across the room. "Jean, you better get your sister before Ellen claws her eyes out."

Sure enough, Lisa flirted not just with Hunter, but with serious danger.

Ellen Boroughs was the same height and build as the girl who'd been making out with Hunter last week. It must have been her. The way she grabbed his shoulder and glowered at

Lisa seemed territorial, at any rate.

Jean swore under her breath and pulled out her phone to type a quick text as Cat took her turn. A second later, Lisa pulled out her phone. She didn't seem to like the message much, judging from the furious look she sent her sister. She jabbed out a comeback and slid the phone back in her pocket.

"Idiot," Jean muttered as she read her text. She took another shot, but her attention went across the room before the ball had a chance to fall into the pocket. "Opinions?"

I shrugged. "I don't know. Our alternate's not bad..."

Cat gave me a faint smile at the compliment. "Yeah, but I don't want on the team because of a death."

Maria frowned at the table, trying to pick a shot. "But if everyone knows Ellen did it, she'll be too busy standing trial to enter the Catscratch."

"Good point," Jean said. "Could be our ticket to Regionals."

But despite the promise of removing our main competition, Jean put away her cue at the end of the game. "I'd better get the brat home. We have family crap in the morning anyway."

"Yeah." Maria put her stick away too. "And I have to go study."

"Study?" I asked. "On a Saturday night?"

"Tell me about it." Maria shook her head. "My parents keep wigging out about my SAT scores."

I stared at her. That was crazy. "Ninety-ninth percentile's not good enough for them?"

"Apparently not." She put an arm around Cat's waist and pecked her cheek. "We're on for tomorrow afternoon though, right?"

Cat's head dropped to Maria's shoulder. "No studying?"

"No. I traded tonight's freedom for tomorrow's."

Cat didn't look happy, but she nodded. "Yeah, alright. Pick me up at noon?"

"Noon it is, my love." Maria gave her a quick squeeze and waved to me and Jean before heading out the door.

"That's insane," Jean said.

"Seriously," Cat muttered. She looked at me. "You running

off too or do you want to play again?"

I shrugged. "I'm up for another game."

Cat moved to rack up and Jean went to grab her sister. Lisa didn't want to go, but stopped shy of throwing a full tantrum in front of Hunter.

"What happened with you two?" Cat asked, leaning against her cue and looking toward Hunter. Ellen slid her chair closer when Lisa left, getting close enough to Hunter that I wondered why she didn't just straddle him.

I plopped the cue-ball onto the table and whacked it toward the other balls. "I thought it was going somewhere. Turned out to be wrong."

"Hmm." She watched as I failed to sink anything. "He's a moron then."

I shook my head with a little smile. "Thanks. I can see why he'd prefer Ellen though."

Cat stopped eying the table and gave Ellen a quick study. "No, you're prettier. Smarter."

"Shorter. Smaller breasted. And still in high school."

"Alright, I'll grant a point for the high school thing." She shrugged. "But it's not like there's a big maturity difference between a high school senior and college freshman."

"No," I agreed. "But there's a massive difference between living with your parents and not."

"True." She finally decided which side she'd rather be and made an easy pocket with the three before sighting up to shoot the five. "But I'm sure he'd get a dorm room if that's where his mind's at."

"Maybe he thinks she's more likely to go into it." Couldn't blame him if he did. It's not like I was the only-after-marriage type, but Ellen... I wouldn't call her a slut or anything like that, but she was certainly active. Whereas I... Well, I was a lot less experienced. And our community was small enough for people to know it.

Cat mumbled an agreement and sunk another ball. "I revert to my statement about him being a moron."

But he was a happy moron. Or so I assumed from the way

he pulled Ellen against him and bent to whisper in her ear.

When I finally got another turn, I wasted it trying a clever shot that failed miserably. Cat didn't say anything as she took over again, but after she sunk the eight she didn't offer to play another game. "Wanna switch to air hockey?"

At least at air hockey I could take the side of the table that faced away from Hunter and Ellen. "Sure. I'll get some more quarters."

I ran over to the coin machine and slid in a dollar bill. It whirled and went beep. I frowned. It wasn't supposed to go beep, it was supposed to go clink-clink as it dropped coins into the little holder. A red light on front started to flash.

"Break it?" Lucas asked.

What was he doing here? Hadn't he got the memo about Burger Land being open?

He pressed a button and the machine beeped again, then spat out my dollar bill. He pocketed it.

"Hey! That's mine!"

His lips twitched at my outburst and he dug into a different pocket. "Chill. I assume you wanted quarters."

The coins were warm as they fell into the palm I held out. A more polite person would have thanked him. I didn't bother.

"So..." He followed me as I started back toward Cat. "Where's the rest of your gaggle?"

I stopped and stared at him. "The rest of my what?"

"Your gaggle. Your pack. Your gang. Your teammates?" He gave me a hopeful look as I took a deep breath and considered jamming his stupid quarters down his throat.

"Gaggle. Like a pack of geese?"

He sighed. "Sorry. I wasn't trying to offend you."

"Whatever." I crossed my arms across my chest and took a step away, but he grabbed my elbow to stop me from getting further.

"Adam said to say hi to Jean."

My eyes flicked to his hand and he moved it. "Lucky for you she's not here so you don't have to lie and say you did it."

He frowned. "I wasn't going to do that. I was going to tell

her. I'm telling you so you can tell her."

"Really?"

He made a light snorting sound and shook his head. "Why do you think I mentioned it?"

"I have no idea, Lucas." I moved again. He let me this time, but he stayed with me.

"Hey, Cat," he called when we got closer. "Do me a favor and let Jean known Adam sends his regards."

"Um." Cat moved her focus between the two of us, clearly confused. "Okay?"

"Thanks." Lucas grinned at her, gave me a nod, and leaned against the wall next to the air hockey machine. Neither of them bothered telling me where they knew each other from. "So how'd you guys do tonight?"

Cat winced.

I scowled. "We won, but it wasn't pretty."

Lucas nodded. "Ah. Gotcha."

"And I'm sure you did great," I muttered.

Cat shook her head at me and took the puck out of its slot.

"Nope," Lucas said, sounding faintly amused. "Lots of bench time for me. And Adam cracked some ribs. That's why he sent me after his sister."

"She's over there," I said, not pausing long enough to think about consoling him.

"What Darcy means is..." Cat said, giving me a look of chastisement.

I rolled my eyes. "Sympathies. I'm close to being benched too."

"You are not." Cat tapped the table with her paddle and gestured toward the coin feeder. "You want winner, Bench Boy?"

I looked down, using paying for the game as an excuse not to look at Lucas. On a scale of one to ten, how rude would it be to scream at him to go away? What was he doing hanging around us anyway? Other than making me nervous?

"Sure," he said. And I started breathing again.

I slammed the coin loader in and the table whirled to life.

Now... Moment of truth. Did I play like usual or did I let Cat win since the winner had to play Lucas?

Seriously, I was tempted to throw the game. I really was. But in the end, I just couldn't do it. That's not the kind of girl I am. It may have been the kind of girl Cat was though. She went down fast and easy. She's usually better than that.

Eyes narrowed, I shook her hand when it was over. Part of me wanted to say something, but another part told me I was being ridiculous. Maybe Cat was off her game because her girlfriend kept running off to study for a test that anyone else would have said they'd already aced. Or maybe it was what that meant. Though Cat was smart enough to get into an Ivy League school, if she had ambitions in that direction she hid them well. Junior year's a little early to be stressing out because your significant other might be going to a different college than you are, but she wouldn't be the first person to do it.

Lucas picked up Cat's mallet and looked at me across the table. The light reflected off his glasses, hiding his eyes. His mouth was drawn in a tight line, like he was already concentrating on my moves.

The extra study didn't do him any good. He lost anyway, even faster than Cat had.

"Wow," he said. "I even suck at air hockey."

Cat smiled at him. "Maybe you should go back to curling."

Huh? I squinted at her. She shrugged and said, "He was at Nationals the same year Charlie was."

Charlie was her older brother. He was as competitive as she wasn't and was on the team we sent to Junior Nationals two years before.

I looked at Lucas, who had taken a sudden and engrossing interest in a sticker plastered to the edge of the air hockey table. He picked at it with a frown, like its existence annoyed him.

"Then what?" I asked. "Decided it was beneath him and quit?"

He glanced up. "No."

I don't know if he would have told me more or not because Carol suddenly yelled his name from across the room.

Lucas, and plenty of other people, looked over at Adam's sister as she moved in our direction, her hips swaying way more than they needed to. "Yeah?"

"I'm ready to go now."

Lucas's gaze flickered to me, but he cleared his throat and moved away from the table. "Promised Adam."

Like he owed me an explanation of why he was leaving before he could educate me on all the things that had made him abandon my favorite sport.

Carol snaked her arm around his. He jumped a little and tried to jerk his arm away, but she held on tight. When she smiled at me, I half-expected to see fangs. "Night, Darcy."

Whatever.

As Carol pulled Lucas away, my eyes caught on something behind them. Hunter leaned against the edge of a table, Ellen nowhere to be seen. His arms were folded across his chest and his short-sleeved tee drew attention to just how good his biceps looked. But it was his eyes that made my breath catch. Because they were locked on me.

HunterStG: Hey, Darcy. Saw you at Petre's earlier. Air hockey?

DarcyCurls: You may now refer to me as Queen of Air Hockey, thank you.

HunterStG: Abandoning curling?

DarcyCurls: Not a chance!

HunterStG: Was worried. Air hockey was Luke's first brush w/ the Dark Side.

DarcyCurls: ???

HunterStG: He used to curl. Was good too.

DarcyCurls: Did everyone know that but me?

HunterStG: We used to be teammates.

DarcyCurls: Really???

HunterStG: Back in MN. He choked and ditched us at Nationals.

DarcyCurls: Ditched you?

HunterStG: Left between games. Said he was sorry. Like that changed things.

DarcyCurls: Wow! Did you have a sub?

HunterStG: Yeah but he sucked. Luke running off lost the spiel for us.

DarcyCurls: What an ass!

HunterStG: In a nutshell.

Chapter Twelve

As the door opened on a chaotic hell, I slammed myself for not insisting Mom pay me more for going through this on her behalf. Over a dozen screaming minions of evil ran shrieking through the room, their voices echoing off of every surface and making me long to plunge a knife into my uterus. No way was I ever having kids if it meant hosting something like this.

The twins ran in at full tilt, their little faces shining with excitement. It'd have been cute if they'd had a mute button.

"Darcy!" Mrs. Tinsley, mother of the birthday girl, beamed at me. She didn't look nearly as frazzled as she should, leaving me fairly certain her huge purse held at least one flask of something not sold by the arcade hosts. "You're such an angel. Your mom is so lucky."

"Thanks. Be sure you tell her that." I smiled and looked around.

"I can take those," Mrs. Tinsley said, grabbing the bags I carried. "Do you know Lucas Fitzwilliam? He's over there."

I looked. If I'd thought about it I might not have, but the statement confused me. Lucas was at this party? Was he friends with kindergarteners? Cause that would be weird.

He was about ten yards away, wearing the new glasses again and a dark brown sweater with a young child clinging to his waist. A girl. She had the same hair he did, except that it tumbled all the way down her back, held in place by a sparkling rhinestone headband.

As Mrs. Tinsley scurried off, I bit my lip and tried to decide what to do. On one hand, all the games here were seriously lame and Lucas was the only other teenager in sight. On the other hand... He was Lucas. He was probably angry at me for beating him last night, in front of Carol no less. And then there was what Hunter messaged me about. Did I want to talk to a guy who'd walked out on his team in the middle of Nationals? What kind of person does that?

Then Lucas looked at me.

I knew the expression on his face. It was the same one I wore. A battered, scared look screaming for help. The look of a rabbit watching a trapper bear down on it, unable to run because of the steel jaws latched into its ankle.

Except Lucas wasn't held in place by metal, he was free to move. And he did, coming straight for me.

"Lulu!" the little girl whined as they approached. "Pick me up!"

Lulu? Lucas closed his eyes for a moment before scooping the child up and whispering something into her ear. She made a gasping sound and put her hand over her mouth. Lucas shook his head and told her, "It's okay. I'm sure my reputation will survive."

He smiled at me, but it was a self-conscious smile.

"Yeah," I said. "Your rep's safe, Lulu."

His arms tightened around the girl.

I held my hand out to the child. "Hey. I'm Darcy."

"Oh!" She reached out to shake my hand, almost tipping out of Lucas's hold. "I'm Amelia Grace Fitzwilliam."

"Nice to meet you." My eyes flickered to Lucas, wondering if he was going to elaborate on his relationship with Amelia. He didn't. "I'm with Daniel and Elijah. I'm their sister."

She nodded, her brown eyes huge. "I'm with my uncle."

"Uncle Lulu?"

She giggled. "You're not supposed to call him that."

"I won't do it again," I said, although I was fairly certain I would. The resignation on Lucas's face told me he thought I would too. If he didn't play his cards right, I'd even call him that in front of other people.

"Teri!" Amelia's cry nearly burst my eardrum. Lucas's ears had to be ringing. His niece squirmed from his grasp, leaping down to run across the room.

Lucas rubbed his ear.

"Nice set of pipes," I said.

"Yeah." He watched her reunite with her friend, a cute dark skinned girl whose pigtails where held up by bright pink ribbons. The two talked with huge hand motions and exaggerated expressions. They were obviously best friends.

"Me and Jean used to be like that." I hadn't expected that to sound sad, but it did. Mournful.

Lucas shook his head. "You and Jean are still like that. Unless you meant short. Jean isn't short anymore."

"But I am?" I plucked my hands on my hips and tried to look menacing. Which wasn't easy considering that Lucas had an entire foot on my height.

"You're petite," he said.

My eyes narrowed. "And Jean isn't? Are you calling my best friend fat?"

His hands went up in front of him, palms toward me. His eyes were big, panicked. It was all I could do not to laugh. As a smile broke through on my face, he lowered his hands and started smiling back. "You're evil."

I grinned. "Yeah, I know."

A horde of rampaging five- and six-year-olds stampeded past, forcing me to back up against a claw machine. Lucas advanced in their wake, coming to stand close beside me, like doing that would mean I could better protect him from the next onslaught.

He half-turned and looked into the case with a frown of consideration. Was he going to play? Would he go for the yellow pants-wearing cube that was in no way Spongebob Squarepants or the spaceman that was similar to but definitely not Buzz Lightyear?

Mrs. Tinsley made her way back to us, still not looking like any of this was getting to her. Clearly, she was stoned off something she was too stingy to share. She smiled in sympathy. "You two don't have to hang around if you don't want to. We've got enough parents to keep things from getting out of hand."

Lucas looked around in disbelief, probably thinking the same thing I was. If this was control, we'd never survive a lack of it.

Mrs. Tinsley laughed. "If you think this is bad, you do not want to be here when the cake comes out."

I shuddered.

"When do you want us back?" Lucas asked.

"Two hours."

I was out the door with him before it registered that he might expect us to hide from the party together. It wasn't like either of us had other plans since we weren't expecting our reprieve. I snuck a look at him from the corner of my eye. He was watching me, but looked away as soon as he saw me notice.

"So..." I said.

"Now what?" he asked.

We stopped and looked at each other.

He cleared his throat. "Guess you want to call Jean or something..."

"Jean's busy." I pulled my phone out and looked at it. Jean and Lisa were entertaining their aunt. Maria and Cat had their lunch date. I didn't want to go home from fear of Mom being mad at me for leaving the twins.

"Are you okay?"

I shoved the phone back into my pocket and looked up. Lucas's eyebrows were drawn together as he frowned at me.

"Why wouldn't I be?" I asked.

His lips parted, then came back together. He answered me with a shrug and shifted his feet a little, but didn't start walking again.

I was all set to stalk away. Then he looked up from the sidewalk. Our eyes met. And before I knew it I was blurting, "We could go get coffee."

"Are you going to pour it on me?"

Was I going to pour it on him? I stared for a second, then

86

decided it wasn't all that unreasonable a question. "Only if you give me a reason."

We smiled at each other.

A frigid wind ripped down the street, bringing me to my senses. I'd just asked Lucas to have coffee with me! Grimey! What was I thinking? But it was too late to undo the damage, so I trotted along with him, hurrying to get inside before we froze.

"The weather's gone crazy," I said as we walked into the coffee house and its warm croissant and coffee scented air embraced us.

"Cold front moving in," he said. "We're going to get some snow soon."

"Yep." I stomped my feet on the mat at the entrance and made my way to the barista, my eyes on the board over her head, reading the current specials.

"The pumpkin's good."

"Yeah, I was thinking about that..." I trailed off with the realization that I wasn't replying to Lucas, but to Hunter, who stood on my left with a sardonic smile playing on his lips. "Hey, Hunter. What's up?"

He shrugged. "Homework. You'd be amazed how hard college math is, even the stuff for liberal arts majors."

On my right, Lucas gave a loud snort. "No she wouldn't. She could tutor you."

I looked over to him. "That was almost a compliment."

"Almost." He grinned for a second before his eyes snagged on Hunter. Whatever he saw made the expression vanish. He stepped forward and ordered a drip coffee. House blend. Black.

Following suit crossed my mind, but as I'm more a fan of the stuff people dump into coffee than of coffee itself, I asked for a caramel latte. I couldn't say exactly why I didn't go ahead and get the pumpkin like I would have if Hunter hadn't said anything. Maybe I was afraid he'd think I'd gotten it because of him. I wouldn't want him thinking he had power over me.

More to waste time without having to talk to either of the boys than anything, I browsed the pastry display. Lucas hovered near the coffee counter, but Hunter came up behind me. "You want anything? My treat?"

"No, I'm not hungry." I wrapped my arms around myself and edged back toward Lucas.

"Are you mad at me?" Hunter whispered. He glanced in Lucas's direction. "You're not on a date, are you?"

"God, no," I said, louder than I meant to. Lucas looked over but didn't say anything that would let me know if he'd heard the question or not. I lowered my voice to normal volume. "Why would I be mad at you?"

He shrugged as Lucas took his unadorned coffee and walked over to a shelf of loaner books. "You really that good at math?"

This time, I was the one shrugging. Lucas shook his head and said, without turning around, "She's completely wrecking the grade curve in AP Calc this semester."

"I am not!"

Lucas turned a smile my way. "So you don't consistently have the highest score in class by at least ten points?"

"No. I mean, I score high, but..." I paused. I didn't outscore everyone by that much. Did I? No wonder Lucas got annoyed at my scores. Everyone probably did, the others were just more polite about it.

Hunter laughed. "Either way, sounds like you're better at this stuff than I am. I could use some help..."

As Lucas continued to browse the shelves, I took a look at what Hunter had spread out on a coffee table under the window. A swath of sunlight lit some really basic equations. "Heh. These are so easy, even Lucas could handle them."

"Not a chance," Lucas said, grabbing a book and bringing it over to the arm chair next to Hunter's. He sprawled into the chair and plopped his feet on the table next to the textbook. His high tops were pretty gross, almost solid gray from their dinginess, though they'd once been plaid and I'd guess blue. "He doesn't want help, he wants someone to do it for him."

Scanning his notebook, I could see why. The guy was clearly lost.

There was a sofa free across the table, but rather than take it, I sat on the floor at the end and pulled Hunter's work over. I didn't have any idea how to start helping someone this clueless, so I flipped to a new page and started over.

I went step-by-step, explaining exactly what I was doing, but when I gave the notebook back for Hunter to try the next one, he stared at it like it was all gibberish. I made him try anyway, but it was obvious nothing I'd said had clicked.

So, yeah, I kind of did wind up doing his work for him. Which wasn't terribly ethical, but was worth it because of the way he smiled at me.

TO: jeansmith@merytonhs.com
FROM: darcybennet@merytonhs.com
SUBJECT: The Weirdest Day

How was your day? Survive the relatives?

My day was weird as anything. You know I was supposed to take the twins to a party, right? Well, Lucas was there with his niece. (She's really cute and sweet and it's hard to believe they're related.) We escaped together for a little while, which would have been strange enough, but then Hunter showed up and joined us.

And... Weird doesn't go far enough to describe it. Did you know that they know each other? That they used to curl together? (Did you know Lucas used to curl? Am I really the last person in Meryton to catch on to that?) And... Well, doesn't that seem strange? They were on a team together in Minnesota and now they both live here?

I should probably ask Hunter what's up with that... Right after I ask him what's up with the way he was looking at me today. Okay, maybe he couldn't keep his eyes off me because I was doing his homework, but he kept leaning over like he was smelling me or something and I lost count of how many times he touched me. But he's the one who's going out with someone else, not me.

What do you think?

Love, D

Chapter Thirteen

"Did he say anything about me?" Jean asked, leaning across the aisle before physics.

I squinted at her. "Who? Lucas or Hunter?"

An exasperated look crossed her face. "Lucas, of course. You know, Adam's best friend?"

"Oh." I shook my head. "No. He didn't say much about anything."

As the teacher walked into the room and went up to the board, Jean leaned back in her seat and folded her arms. "He's pretty strange."

"If you think he's strange, wait until you get to San Diego." Even though she hadn't been accepted yet, she was wearing a zippered University of California hoodie that I was trying not to notice. It was driving me crazy though, that hoodie.

She ignored me and watched Mr Rodriguez write some equations up front. "Why didn't he leave if he wasn't going to talk to either of you?"

"Guess he delights in being a third wheel." Not that Hunter and I would have done anything different if he hadn't been there. I didn't think... Hunter had been seriously lost.

"Yeah, he does, doesn't he?" She turned her head back to me and twirled a strand of hair around her finger. Her eyes narrowed in a way I really didn't like.

Foreboding crawled up my spine. "What?"

"Do you think he'd like being a fourth wheel?"

I sat up straight and opened my notebook. "I don't like the way you're looking at me right now."

She turned further, putting legs into the aisle and leaning over them. "You know, if we were all going to the Winter Waltz together, like a group, maybe Colin would back off from you."

"Or decide he's part of our group."

She shrugged. "That's better than going alone with him, isn't it?"

I glared at her. "Except I wasn't going alone with him anyway. No matter what my mom says."

"Your mom?" She frowned, distracted from hounding me for a second.

I shrugged and starting copying the equations as though I couldn't care less about our discussion. I sincerely hoped no one was paying attention to us. "Yeah, she thinks I shouldn't be turning down perfectly acceptable dates when I don't have any other offers."

Jean made an annoyed sound. But then she gasped happily. "But this solves that too. Just tell her you're going with Lucas and leave out the part where it's a group thing."

"Miss Smith," Mr. Rodriguez said. "You'll be needing to have these memorized for the test Thursday. I'd recommend you at least look at them."

Blushing at the scattered laughter, Jean got out her notebook and started scribbling. But between lines, she shot me pleading looks that I didn't even have to look at her to be aware of.

I sighed as I finished the last equation. "Why don't you just ask Adam?"

Jean shook her head and kept writing. "He's scared of commitment."

"Commitment?" I flipped a page in my notebook, wanting to keep the equations separate from the rest of the day's notes to make cramming easier. "Who's talking about commitment? It's a school dance!"

"A formal one. With expensive tickets and fancy clothes." She sighed and stared at the board for a few moments. "It's kind of a couples' thing."

"Would you mind telling that to my mother?"

She laughed. "Wouldn't help. She thinks you should have a boyfriend and would want to know what's wrong with Colin."

As if that wasn't obvious to anyone who'd met him.

I fell silent as Mr. Rodriquez started talking about the things he'd written, telling us when and how to use them. Not all of them were in the text book, so I had to pay attention until he gave us time to work some example problems.

The problems were easy since he'd given us the right equations to use for all of them, so I finished quickly. As I waited for Jean to get hers done, I watched her and wondered why she suddenly kept wanting me to do things I didn't want to do. At what point had her vision for the future become so much more important than my mental and emotional well-being? When she finally put down her pencil, I leaned closer and whispered, "What would you tell the guys? If I did agree?"

She looked at me with big puppy dog eyes.

"No."

"Please?" she asked, drawing the word out.

I shook my head. It was more than just my agreement with Lucas not to interfere with her and Adam, it was the principal of the thing. She wanted me to not only do something I didn't want to do, but to set it up. And she was asking it after acknowledging that who you went to this stupid dance with meant something. Were my feelings even slightly important to her anymore? "No. I'll go along with it if they will, but I'm not asking them."

Her shoulders slumped. "But..."

"Miss Bennet," Mr. Rodriguez called. "Could you demonstrate the first problem for us?"

Swallowing my emotions, I nodded. "Of course."

"You think you don't need me," I hissed to Jean as I got up. "Prove it."

"Who says I don't need you?" Tears shimmered in her eyes.

I met her eyes, then looked down at her shirt. "The University of California."

93

I stalked to the front of the room before she had the chance to say anything. Not that she wanted to say anything. If she had, then she wouldn't have stormed out of the classroom the second the bell rang.

As I trudged into the hall after everyone else, my feet felt heavy and straightening my shoulders would have taken more energy than I could possibly muster. I shoved my way to my locker, ignoring the protests of the people who'd been blocking it.

It had been years since I'd been this upset with Jean. She agreed my mom was wrong to pressure me to go out with Colin, but then she turned around and did the exact same thing with Lucas! If she'd wanted me to ask Adam for her, I would have rolled my eyes, then done it. This though... What right did she have to act all hurt that I didn't want to set up a double-date with someone I didn't like? Didn't she realize that just going along with the plan would be a major sacrifice?

Besides, the dance was the night before the Catscratch Bonspiel. We needed sleep a lot more than we needed boys if we were going to grab that spot for Regionals. Why wasn't my skip more worried about that? Had she forgotten us in favor of California already?

There was an ominous thunk beside me, followed by Colin's extremely unwanted voice. "What's wrong, pussycat?"

My fingers dug into the metal sides of my locker as I closed my eyes and took a long breath. "I don't want to talk about it."

"You sure?"

He lounged against the locker next to mine, his arms folded loosely over his chest. If it wasn't for the way his eyes lingered around my breasts, I might have thought he actually cared.

"Well, there's you," I said. It was meaner than I liked to be, but between the argument with Jean and the racket of the hallway, my nerves were frayed. "What do you want?"

He widened his eyes, playing at being hurt. "I'm just worried about you."

I sighed. "Well, you should be worried about you and your delusions. I never said I'd go to the Waltz with you. Why are

94

you telling people I did?"

The warning bell rang and I swung my locker shut as Colin frowned at me. The confusion wrinkling his face looked genuine, but if it was he'd have to be a complete idiot. "Can we talk at lunch?"

I shook my head. "There's nothing to talk about. I'm sorry, but I don't want to go to the dance."

He followed me as I started walking. "You don't want to go with me?"

Gah! Maybe he was just that stupid. "I don't want to go at all. With anyone. And I'm already fighting with Jean about it, I don't want to debate it with you too."

"Okay..." He looked stricken enough that I felt kind of bad. Unfortunately, he didn't have the sense to leave it at that. "What do you want to do then?"

"What?"

He smiled at me, though it didn't touch his eyes at all. "What do you want to do instead?"

I stopped walking and someone bumped into me. I gave her a quick apology and then stared at Colin. What was I supposed to say? "Nothing."

"You just want to hang? That's cool. I can do that."

"No."

"No?" His voice sounded confused, but his face was smooth. He understood me, he just didn't want to.

"No," I repeated before turning and walking into government. I was worried he'd follow, but for once he did the smart thing.

"Arg," I growled, throwing my books onto my desk. It wasn't until after I'd slammed down into my seat that I noticed Lucas sitting across the aisle. The day just kept getting worse. I slumped down and glowered at the board, silently daring him to say something.

He waited until the bell rang, then tossed a note onto my desk. It was folded up into a little triangle and had my name written in a girlie script.

"What's this?"

"It's a note," he said as the teacher made her way to the front of the room. "Old fashioned, but she didn't have your number to text."

"She who?"

He shrugged. "Read it."

Whatever. I unfolded the paper and nearly laughed at what I saw. "Hey, Darcy! Are you going to the dance with Colin? Text me yes or no. -Scarlet."

Lucas's profile didn't give me any clues about how he came to be the messenger for this little flashback to elementary school communications. I caught his eye and he shot me a questioning look.

"Do you know what this says?" I whispered as I sent a quick denial to the number under Scarlet's signature.

He shook his head. "Should I?"

"Why did you have it?"

He slouched down in his chair and looked forward again. "Wrong place, wrong time."

At the front of the room, the teacher gave me the evil eye, so I gave up on Lucas and started taking notes on the concept of due process for the duration.

The second I left the classroom, Scarlet pounced on me.

"Can I ask him?" she asked.

"Sure." Not that I understood why she'd want to, but I wished her luck. Lots of it. I didn't want to be forced to kill him, they probably don't have curling sheets in prison.

I grabbed her elbow as she started off. "Hold on a sec."

"Yeah? What?" Her head tilted as she watched me.

"Why did you give the note to Lucas?"

She shrugged. "He's the one who told me to write it."

"Really?" That was interesting.

"Yeah," she said. She glanced around the hallway like she was looking for spies. "I was talking to Trish about how I was going to ask Colin after the party, but then he asked you before I got up the nerve. And Lucas popped up and said that was just a rumor. He said I should just ask Colin to the dance, but of course I said that wouldn't be right. So he said I should ask you."

"Uh huh." I nodded, only half following her words. It didn't surprise me that Lucas had been eavesdropping. He did that all the time. But why was this topic one he cared enough about to contribute to the conversation? Not once, but at least twice. Because he'd interrupted me and Jean talking about Colin too.

If the boy in question were anyone other than Lucas, I'd be tempted to think this was a sign of interest in me. But I knew him too well to think that. He made it clear way back at the beginning of the year, when he first moved here, that I wasn't his type. I was a short, smart brunette. He liked Barbie dolls. Lonely Barbie dolls. I was pretty sure his ideal woman had no friends. Or if she had them, they were nothing like any of my friends...

Scarlet fell silent and I realized she'd asked a question. She was watching me with a hopeful smile and clutched hands. Uh... I made a guess about which way I should answer the question I hadn't heard. "Sure."

She grinned. "Thanks, Darcy! You're awesome!"

And she bounced off to tell her friends what I'd said. I hoped I'd given my blessing to her trying to snag Colin and not to something else.

TO: darcybennet@merytonhs.com
FROM: scarletjackson@merytonhs.com
Subject: Thank you!

I asked Colin like you said I should and he said yes!

But... Are you sure that's okay? I can't imagine why you didn't want to go with him yourself... Unless maybe you're wanting to go with someone else? Should I try to guess who?

TO: scarletjackson@merytonhs.com
FROM: darcybennet@merytonhs.com
Subject: RE: Thank you!

There's no one else. I just have a lot on my mind right now and the dance is the night before an important curling tournament, so I'd have to leave early even if I went.

I'm glad you're going. Hope you have a blast!

-Darcy

Chapter Fourteen

Jean's ignoring me should have ended when we met up to curl on Saturday, but it didn't. Not really. We played together, but our conversations consisted of one-word shot calls and the occasional glower. It was killing me, twisting up my insides and making them ache. But what was I supposed to do? Beg to be allowed to ask out someone I didn't even like in the hopes it would help her? No. I wasn't going to grovel for forgiveness for not letting myself be used. I couldn't believe she was trying to force me to.

A crowd gathered at the windows upstairs to watch us lose, which we did by a blowout. We conceded the game down eight after six ends and tried not to listen to the whispers circulating around us as we left the building.

Jean stayed at the other end of the group from me as we rushed through the mandatory socializing at Petre's. I left her there after gulping a slice of pizza that hit my stomach like an oily rock.

Hunter and Ellen were crossing the parking lot as I walked out. He had his arm around her shoulders and the setting sun was bringing out the red highlights in her hair. Neither of these things were right. My shoulders were the ones that needed holding. And the sun should have set long ago, bringing the night. I wanted the night even more than I wanted Hunter, I wanted to sink into the dark and hide forever.

Damn. It had finally happened. I'd gone emo.

Hunter said my name as I passed, but I kept going. The unofficial rules of curling said I had to be civil to the people I played with and against. They didn't say anything about boys who led me on and then paraded around draped over other people when my week was already miserable.

I stopped at my car and rooted through my coat pockets for my keys. It took me a while because they'd fallen through a hole in the lining. And then I dropped them on the pavement, fumbling because of the footfalls pounding the ground behind me.

"Darcy!" Hunter called. "Wait a sec!"

I pressed the button to unlock the car with a pleasant beep, but Hunter closed the distance between us before I could get in and drive off. I turned to him with a sigh. "What's up?"

A couple of snowflakes drifted down. Any other week, they would have made me happy.

"I'm undefeated." He gave me a big smile. Like the snow, it didn't have the usual affect. Instead of getting all bubbly, my insides stayed in their funk.

"Congrats." I opened the front door.

His hand lashed out to grip the top of the door.

Not able to leave anyway, I leaned against the door with my arms folded over the top next to Hunter's hand. Again, it didn't have the affect I would have expected. My skin should have been tingling, even with the layers of air and clothing between it and his fingers. But there was nothing.

Hunter watched me, his eyes roaming over my face as the tips of his hair flicked in the wind. "I didn't see much of your game."

I dropped my eyes down to my coat sleeves. "You didn't miss anything worth watching."

"You know there's some practice ice open tomorrow." The car door shifted as he let go of it. "I'd be happy to work with you if you want. Pay you back for the math help."

I shrugged. Practice wasn't going to help my problem, but maybe it would make me feel better to be out on the ice and not getting glared at. "Yeah. Maybe."

His fingers wrapped around my chin, warm despite the cold air. He tipped my head up and before I could process his intentions, he leaned over the door and pressed his lips against mine.

The kiss was hot. It was thorough and unhurried. It was everything it should have been. Except for the voice in the back of my head screaming about Ellen. And except for the numbness everywhere save my lips. When I'd imagined kissing Hunter, I'd felt it through my whole body, making everything tingle and burn like my skin was being lavished with ice. But, of course, I imagined it without the car door between us. Or the girlfriend across the street. Without those two things, I would have enjoyed it a lot more.

Nauseated by guilt, I turned my head from Hunter and my eyes fell on the parking lot at Petre's. Where Lucas Fitzwilliam stood staring at me.

"I'll call you in the morning," Hunter said, like nothing had happened.

I sat as he left, turned so my feet rested on the asphalt. My elbows jammed into my knees and my head crashed down into my hands. Feeling numb and stupid, I watched the snow fall onto my sneakers and melt.

I looked up again only when a second pair of sneakers came into my limited view. Lucas was close enough that if he'd crossed the street to kill me, I would have been dead before I had time to blink. He didn't look like he wanted to kill me. His mouth was soft and his eyes calm, though his eyebrows came a little closer to each other than usual. No, he didn't look murderous. What he looked was worried.

"What should I do?" I asked, my lips still tingling from Hunter's kiss. I wouldn't have asked that if I'd thought about what I was going to say, but I skipped that phase and just blurted the question out.

His focus didn't shift even a fraction off my face. "About what?"

I looked down to the ground again. The wind was blowing the snow at a slight angle and Lucas was completely shielding me from it now. I couldn't answer the question, couldn't put the answer into words. "You know about what. Don't make me say it."

The car beside mine gave a slight clink as Lucas leaned against it. I hoped the metal on his pockets wasn't going to damage its paint. "Is the argument about Adam?"

Huh? "Me and Hunter looked like we were arguing?"

He snorted. "No. But you and Jean did. Have all week."

"Oh." I let out a breath. It turned into a pretty white cloud that slithered to Lucas's legs. "It was a little bit about Adam."

"I'm sorry."

I glanced up at him. His face was turned so I couldn't see his expression. He started to turn more toward me and I dipped my head again. "It's only part your fault. And mostly California's."

"California's? Who's California?"

My lips curled up and I shook my head. "It's a where. Big state over by the Pacific Ocean. South of Oregon. North of Mexico."

"Right. The place with all the earthquakes? I can see how somewhere like that could cause arguments."

"She's going to school there," I said, my voice scarcely more than a whisper. For a few seconds I'm not sure he was able to hear me, then he whistled softly.

"I'm sorry, Darce. That sucks."

"Yeah, I know." I swallowed, holding back the tears that wanted to spill by grabbing onto the anger thinking about being abandoned brought. My teeth grit together and warmth spread across the back of my neck.

"No chance of you going with her?"

His hands went up in a warding gesture as I glared up at him.

"I'll take that as a no."

"Do that," I said. I probably sounded angry, but I think he knew it wasn't directed at him. I shook my head as I tried to calm down a little. "The only dedicated curling ice on the entire West Coast is way up in Seattle."

I expected him to say something about how I could live with arena ice for four years, but he didn't. He showed more insight than that. "So she's changing her plans, which changes yours."

"Yeah."

He stood slowly and took a step closer to me. "And you don't think she should have done that without asking you."

I shake my head. "I know you mean that it's a bad thing, me feeling that way. But it's not any more selfish than her walking out on me."

"Walking out on you?" He sighed. "You do know she's your friend, right? Not your wife."

"Screw you." In a flash, I twisted to get my feet in the car and my hand on the door handle, but Lucas got in the way before I could slam the door. I considered doing it anyway, but made the mistake of looking at him.

His face was soft with sympathy, his eyes open and honest. I hated him in that instant, but I moved my hand from the door and let him brace himself in the opening. He leaned into the car, the light scent of body wash coming with him. "All I meant was that she'll still be your friend. Even if she's in California."

"Yeah, I know." I drew my legs up in front of me, pressing my shins into the steering wheel. "But ever since we were little, we were going to Catskill together."

If he'd told me that people change, I would have shoved his ass onto the roadway and drove off. But he didn't. "And you're going to Catskill still? No matter what?"

My voice caught when I tried to speak, so I just nodded.

"You know I'm going to Catskill, right?" His lips jerked up a little.

I looked at him for a second, then started smiling back. "Still not enough to get me to California."

"No." He hair flopped forward as he moved in closer. "Seattle's looking better though, isn't it?"

"Maybe."

He yanked himself upright all of sudden and took a step back. A strange expression crossed his face, one I couldn't read. "About the other thing..."

103

I sighed. "I didn't refuse to help her with Adam because of you. I just didn't want to do something she asked me to do."

He hesitated for a second. "What... Never mind. You shouldn't do whatever it is if you don't want to. But that's not what I meant."

He'd backed up far enough that snow was falling into the car. It was sticking on the ground already. When full dark fell, there'd be some accumulation. Lucas took a deep breath and inched forward.

"What?" I asked.

"Hunter... He's..." Lucas shook his head. "He's not the most reliable of people."

I laughed. It was harsh and grating and ugly. "And I know how much value you place on reliability."

He frowned, confused for a second. Then his eyes popped open with the realization of what I meant. "He told you about Nationals."

"Yeah." One arm was draped over my knees as I turned to scowl. "He told me how you left your team in the middle of them."

His jaw was tight and his expression cold as he met my eyes. He held my gaze for a long moment, his glistening with intensity. "Did he tell you why?"

His voice made me want to shiver. It wasn't just cold, it was dead. "It doesn't matter. There's nothing that could justify that."

He shook his head, his mouth twisted into a parody of his earlier smile. "I wish I had as little imagination as you do."

Then he turned and stalked back to Petre's.

WHAT TO DO ABOUT HUNTER

1. Rat him out to Ellen. I mean, obviously they're together. Although maybe she doesn't care because they aren't exclusive and I'll just make a fool out of myself.

2. Ask him what he meant. (Yeah, right!)

3. Ignore him forever.

4. Throw myself at him.

5. ???

TO: cnetherfield@sotc.com
FROM: darcybennet@myrtonhs.com
SUBJECT: Lucas Fitzwilliam

Hey, Cat! I was just wondering... Do you have any idea why Lucas left Nationals? Because I mentioned it to him today and he got really weird. Hunter implied that there wasn't a reason, he just left. But I think I'm missing something.

-D

TO: darcybennet@myrtonhs.com
FROM: cnetherfield@sotc.com
SUBJECT: Lucas Fitzwilliam

I have no idea why he left. Sorry. I'll ask my brother, but I don't know that he'd know either.

As for what you're missing... I'm not sure. But I can tell you that Hunter and Lucas do not get along. At all. You have noticed how they can't be in the same room without giving each other serious stink-eye, right?

I'll let you know what Charlie says.

Meow! -Cat

Chapter Fifteen

Although I went to sleep obsessing over Hunter and remembering the feel of his lips on mine, it was Lucas who invaded my dreams. We were in the club, on sheet three. He was in full hockey gear, including skates, and was ripping up the ice by skating up and down the sheet around the rocks I was throwing. He had his stick down, holding it like a broom, but he wasn't sweeping the ice so much as shaving it.

"You're thinking too much," he said, destroying the space before the hack with a showy hockey stop that sprayed slivers of ice over me. "Remember what Yoda said."

"May the Force be with you?"

He rolled his eyes and clunked his stick against the top of the rock I was lining up to throw. "No. Do or do not. There is no try. There's also no think. Just do it."

"That's Nike, not Yoda."

"Whatever." He hopped over the border, onto the next sheet over where a hockey match had started and I was left to stare at the mess he'd made of my ice.

My phone woke me with a signal that I had a text and I rolled over to check who it was from. For a second, I thought it was Jean. Then I remembered we weren't talking to each other and my heart sort of nosedived.

It was Hunter's name on the screen when I toggled my phone on. "Ice open @ 11. You in?"

It took me a while to answer because I really didn't know

what my answer was. The whole Hunter situation had gotten more complicated than I wanted to deal with. But I was off my game and could use help. And it wasn't like he'd do anything at the club, not with all the people who'd be around. So, I texted that I'd see him at eleven and dragged myself into the shower before heading over.

When he still hadn't shown by eleven thirty, I claimed an empty sheet by myself and started some solo training. Although calling it training is generous. Mostly all I did was make bad throw after bad throw. And, of course, the more I tried to correct myself, the more I sucked.

After sending all sixteen rocks down the sheet without being happy with one of them, I slid to the far side to start again. I took a break though, sitting on the bench and watching the activities on the other sheets. My fellow curlers went on, oblivious.

Maybe my subconscious wasn't just trying to make sure I woke up in a pissy mood when it sent me a dream about Lucas. Maybe what he'd said was what I needed to work on. Maybe I was thinking too much. That would certainly explain why I got worse the more effort I exerted.

I resolved to think less and got up to send the rocks back to the start. The returns weren't much better, but they felt more natural. I stopped over-analyzing and let myself just play.

Unfortunately, I still had a problem even if I had less of one than I did when I started.

As I started sliding the rocks into place for the next people to come along, the door to the warm room opened and Hunter strolled in. I glanced at the clock. Half past noon.

"Hey, Darcy." He grinned at me, not looking at all apologetic for being late. "Sorry, I got held up."

"No big." I shrugged and took the ice-cleaning broom down from the wall.

"Hold up on that," Hunter said, trotting over. "I think I saw your problem from upstairs."

I paused. "Oh?"

"Yeah." He took the broom from me and put it back on its

108

hanger. "You're pushing out on your release."

"What? Really?" Just before releasing the rock, an advanced curler will do something we call a positive release. It's sort of a little push. But it's essential that you not push out, which is pushing in a direction other than the target.

"Afraid so," Hunter said.

Easy enough to test if that was the problem. I slid out one of the rocks and took another practice shot, concentrating on keeping my wrist aligned right. Even though I didn't have much faith in doing better than before, the stone moved in a perfect line and stopped just inside the house. Pretty close to perfect.

Hunter gave me a knowing look when I straightened.

"Thanks," I said.

"Thanks?" He stepped in close to me. "Is that all I get? There are people who get paid to make observations like that."

I smiled a little. "Yeah, but you're not one of them."

He reached out and grabbed my hand. The hairs on my arm stood up and my chest tightened. I reminded myself that I didn't want him to kiss me again, because of Ellen. It didn't matter whether this kiss would be more electrifying than the one before, the one where the car door was interfering. "I'm sorry I was late. I have half an hour before I'm supposed to help with Little Rocks though..."

His eyes made it clear that he wasn't offering to spend that time curling. But I ran from what I saw there, taking my hand back though I stayed smiling. "Then it's your shot."

He shook his head, but went along with me.

Part of me hoped I'd go back to sucking, but I didn't. I threw four stones straight into the heart of the house before sliding up the ice to throw them back again.

The second I turned to look back toward the front of the club, my lack of breakfast hit me and I was suddenly bobbing on a wave of nausea. I swallowed hard and chastised myself for not eating. And the sick feeling had to be from skipping food. Because if it wasn't that, it was the fact that Lucas was staring at me.

I could hardly see him because of the angle of the lights hitting the glass, but somehow I knew his eyes where trailing me as I lined up and I was pretty sure he smiled when I looked up.

The shot was even closer to perfect than the ones before it.

I looked up to see how Lucas reacted, but he wasn't watching me anymore. He was looking down at the small form of his niece. He was definitely smiling.

"Good shot," Hunter said, not acting like he noticed my distraction.

He slid a rock of his own down, taking mine out.

"Meanie," I said.

He grinned at me. "You're the one who wanted to play."

True. He'd sounded like he wanted to play too, but he'd had a different game in mind. "Can I ask you something?"

I swept the bottom of my next stone while he frowned down at me.

"I don't know," he said slowly. "When girls use that tone, I usually don't like the question much."

"So you don't want me to ask questions about Ellen, then?"

He took a long breath. "I'd rather you didn't."

"Fair enough." Except it wasn't, was it? He had something going with her and he wanted to have something going with me. That gave me a right to ask about her.

The rock I sent while thinking about that didn't do as well as its friend did. It slid through the house, missing Hunter's rock by several inches.

"You pushed out again," he said.

I shrugged. I hadn't really been trying with that shot.

Out in the warm room, Lucas was back to watching us, holding Amelia up so she could get a good look too. She held one of those cute little brooms the Little Rockers use and when she twisted to say something to her uncle, she nearly clocked him with the broom handle.

I tried on my next two shots. They were draws, not take-outs. Each one curled around Hunter's stones perfectly, letting him guard me. If he'd had fewer rocks out there, he'd have been able to knock his guards into mine and take them out. But the ice was too crowded for that to work.

"Can you clean up?" he asked, looking a little pissed although his voice was level. "I have to talk to Lynn."

"Sure. Thanks for the help."

I shook my head as he went to find the Little Rocks coordinator. Maybe he had something real to talk to her about. I hoped so since the alternative was that he was a complete jerk.

The ice cleaned, I opened the door to the warm room. The blast of sound from all the little kids waiting to curl made me want to slam the door shut and stay on the ice. But since they'd be coming that way any minute, I darted instead to the locker room and changed my shoes like I'd been blessed with super speed.

Rushing blindly, I slammed into Lucas on my way out the door.

He smiled. "Kids spook you a lot for someone who lives with them."

"The twins are why kids scare me, Lulu." I sidestepped to get around him, but he turned to walk with me.

"You looked better today," he said as I rushed out into the parking lot. The sudden sunlight made me stop and blink as my eyes adjusted. I guess it made me look confused because he went on to say, "I was at the game last night. Amelia wanted to see it."

"Why?" I held my hand up to shield my eyes and squinted at him, uncertain why I was having this conversation.

He shrugged. "Her mom used to curl. Your brothers told her you did and she wanted to see."

"Why didn't her mom bring her?"

Even though there wasn't a cloud in the sky, his face was suddenly shadowed. "Her mom's dead."

Oh... "She was your sister?"

"Yeah."

Oh...

"Don't." He folded his arms and shook his head at the

111

ground. "Don't say it."

"It?"

"Whatever you were going to say. I've heard it before and it doesn't help."

I wasn't sure what I'd been going to say, but he was probably right on both counts. He walked back into the building before I could think of a response.

CATSKILL COLLEGE APPLICATION

PERSONAL ESSAY

OPTION 3: THE MOST IMPORTANT THING IN MY LIFE IS...

The most important thing in my life is curling. Curling has taught me the power of perseverance. Just because an end is lost doesn't mean you can give up on the game. And losing a game doesn't mean you can declare the season over.

At the same time, curling teaches us realism. There does come a point when you stop fighting. Curling is one of the few sports in which it's perfectly acceptable to concede defeat. In fact, outside of purely social games, it's considered rude not to concede if there's no reasonable chance that you'll win.

At first glance, the last two paragraphs may seem contradictory. But they aren't really. The key to perseverance is knowing when to utilize it and when to give up for today so that you can fight tomorrow.

How does this apply to my life off the ice?

Um... Good question.

I'm full of crap, aren't I?

Right. So I'll delete this draft of this stupid essay just like all the others and hope that the English paper I have to spend the rest of the day writing sucks less.

Chapter Sixteen

Monday was disappointing in its predictability. The ten page English paper I wasted half of Sunday on didn't save us from having a quiz on the reading that none of us had time for since we were all writing essays. I got called on in calculus for a problem I didn't know how to solve, which had Lucas frowning at me like I'd forgotten how to spell my name. And I was late for lunch and all they had left was corn dogs, which I hated.

By the time I made it to the team practice the league coordinator had called on my team's behalf, I wanted to go hide under my bed. In theory, Steph was a coach for all of the junior girls teams at Catskill. In reality, she worked with Team Nemesis, AKA her daughter's team, and told the rest of us she was busy with administration. Of all times for her to decide to pay attention to me, she had to pick the day from hell.

"What's up with this?" she asked. We were in the locker room, fighting reluctance to get our shoes changed. The room seemed more cramped than usual and it had never seemed particularly spacious. It didn't feel like there was enough oxygen in the area to support my entire team, let alone the team plus Steph.

"With what?" Lisa asked, giving her a sullen look. "With Miss I'm Going To Kill Myself Because I Missed a Question on my SATs or with the feuding lesbos?"

"Lesbos?" Maria snarled. She jumped off her bench and crossed the yards between her and our lead. Her hands clenched into fists and her arms trembled in visible spasms. "What the hell do you mean by that?"

Not seeming to realize that she was on the verge of getting her teeth knocked out, Lisa rolled her eyes. "Not like lesbians. Like codependent freaks."

The answer didn't do anything to placate Maria. She towered over Lisa, and if Lisa had possessed any sense at all she would have started groveling for forgiveness. "That is not what the word means, you frigging brat."

"Enough," Steph said, putting her hand on Maria's shoulder. "No more name calling. Any of you."

Maria jerked away and stomped into the bathroom, slamming the door behind her.

My mouth opened, but I couldn't think of anything to say.

Steph took a deep breath. "Obviously, Maria's a little stressed out over college. What's wrong with the rest of you?"

No one said anything. Not even Lisa, though I expected something obnoxious out of her.

"Girls..."

I folded my arms and leaned back against the wall as Steph tried to give us a penetrating adult look. The problem was, she more closely resembled a chipmunk than anything menacing. As mom-looks went, hers was seriously underpowered.

"Fine," she said. "Don't tell me."

She waited a moment while we did what she said.

"Go home."

"What?" Jean asked, startled into speaking.

"Go. Home." Suddenly Steph's expression did seem a little frightening. "Going out on the ice isn't going to do any good if you won't even look at each other."

She paused, clearly expecting us to start looking now. We didn't.

"Right," she said. "You have one week before the bonspiel. Get over yourselves or forfeit."

My spine straightened. "Forfeit? Seriously?"

"Forfeit. Seriously."

She followed Maria into the bathroom while the rest of us

115

sat in shock.

"Whatever," Lisa said. She hadn't changed her shoes yet, so she just picked up her coat and left.

I sat and stared at my feet, listening to the rustling sound of Jean switching back to street shoes. I wanted to say something, but what? I still wasn't willing to apologize for not acting like a good little servant and what else was there to do?

CATSKILL COLLEGE APPLICATION

PERSONAL ESSAY

OPTION 3: THE MOST IMPORTANT ACTIVITY IN MY LIFE IS...

The most important activity in my life is curling because even when everyone in my life abandons me, the ice is there. My family can ignore me. My teachers can harass me. My friends can turn their backs. My teammates can stab me through the heart. But as long as the freezers stay on, the ice remains.

The ice is my home. The echo of sounds off it is music. Its smell soothes my soul. The cold against my skin is like a balm. It's the place I love most in the world.

Chapter Seventeen

If anything, Tuesday was worse than Monday. Plagued by nightmares, I'd hardly slept the night before and by the time study hall rolled around all I wanted to do was lay my head on my desk and take a nap.

Facing away from the window, I lowered my head onto my folded arms and let my eyes drift shut.

The chair beside me squeaked. It's were Jean usually sat, but the footsteps proceeding the squeak hadn't been hers.

"You okay?" Lucas asked.

"Peachy," I mumbled.

"No, really..."

I turned my head, even though that meant more light shining against my eyelids.

The bell rang and all around the room people settled down. I had the feeling Lucas was staring at my hair. It made my scalp itch.

"Darcy," he said, not getting the message that I wanted to be left alone. "Look... About Jean..."

With a grunt, I sat up and stared blearily at him. "Even if I wanted to talk about Jean, what makes you think I'd want to discuss her with you?"

He sat there with his mouth slightly open for a minute before finally saying, "Sorry. I... Sorry."

He got up and moved.

I felt a little bad about it. But mostly I felt exhausted, so I lay my head down again. My eyes didn't close the whole way though, they narrowed to slits and watched Lucas as he crossed the room and put his stuff down over there. This time, he chose the desk next to Jean.

She looked surprised when she noticed him. Or her shoulders did. He was on the far side of her, so she faced away from me as he talked to her.

Not being able to read lips, I couldn't tell what he was saying. He spoke slowly, hesitantly. Quietly enough that his voice didn't carry across the aisles, but loud enough Jean didn't seem to have trouble listening. His eyes kept shying away from her, frequently moving my way. I kept still and hoped he couldn't tell I wasn't asleep.

Whatever he was saying, it wasn't easy for him. He was so nervous I was nearly squirming on his behalf.

Jean sat perfectly still as Lucas spilled whatever he was spilling.

When he finally fell silent she turned her head slowly and looked over at me. My eyelashes hid the details of her expression.

Lucas said something else and Jean nodded.

Then she smiled.

And then she got up, walked around her desk, and hugged him.

At which point I buried my head against my forearm, tried to pretend I hadn't seen that, and tried even harder not to cry.

I didn't look up again until the end of the period.

Jean was standing over me when I did.

"Hey," she said. "Morning, Sunshine."

Slowly, I sat up and wiped the side of my cheek. It didn't feel like I'd been drooling, but it's best to be safe about that kind of thing.

"So..." She perched on the desk next to mine, gripping its sides with her hands and staring down at her pink high-tops. "Lucas told me what he made you promise."

I grunted. My eyes went to where he'd been earlier, but he was long gone. So was everyone else, including the teacher. I got up and stretched. The clock said I had two minutes to get to my next class, but I wasn't sure how accurate it was.

"Yeah," Jean said. "This fight's about more than that, isn't it?"

"Yeah." I nodded. "It is."

There were tears in my eyes as I turned and walked away. Didn't get more than five feet. I would have kept going, but Jean sobbed and I froze. I didn't turn around though. If I turned around, I would have run over and wrapped my arms around her. And I didn't want to do that. She told me what Lucas had said like she'd forgiven me. But she was the one who needed to ask forgiveness.

She gave a loud, ugly sniff. "Darcy... I hate leaving you. I don't want to do it before I have to."

A jolt of hatred went through me. "You don't have to leave. You want to leave."

"Darcy!"

I made it another yard or two before stopping again. "What, Jean? What do you want from me?"

"I want you to be my friend. My best friend." Her footsteps moved over the carpet behind me. "I know it's dramatic, but I feel like I'm going to die if I stay here. I... I need to get out. To be me. To find out who I am when I'm not in the same town my family's been in since before the Revolutionary War."

I took a jagged breath. "You're right. That is dramatic. Just like a really bad, really boring, really poorly scripted movie."

"I'm sorry," she whispered.

My shoulders shook as I balled my hands around the strap of my satchel. "Yeah, me too."

One foot. One yard. Two yards. I was almost to the door.

I stopped. I had to be sure she understood how what she said applied to me. "When you say you need to get away from here, Jean... I'm part of here. And I'm happy to be part of here."

"I know."

The last few intact bits of my heart crumbled apart.

The bell rang and suddenly we were late and suddenly it

seemed okay for me to lose hold of the tears I'd been fighting.

"Darcy..." I could hear her walking up to me, but I still couldn't look at her. "It's great that you're happy here. I love that about you. I really do. But I'm not you."

I wiped my hand against my eyes, smearing tears over my face. "But California? Can't you be in New York? Or Boston? Or, hell, Jean, anywhere on the East Coast?"

Her foot thumped against a chair leg, rhythmically, like she was thinking hard about what to say. "You remember when my parents first split up? And Dad had that place across town?"

"Yeah..." I turned around. Where was this going?

"Remember how many times Lisa sneaked out of our house and went over to his?"

"Like once or twice a week."

"Right." She grabbed my hands and held them in hers, looking at me with eyes bright with emotion. "And how many times did she do that after he went to Kansas City?"

"Never." I sniffled. "Cause who wants to live in Kansas City?"

She shook her head. "It wasn't because she doesn't like Missouri. It was because he'd finally really left."

There was a huge lump in my throat as I swallowed. "And you think you have to go to California to really leave?"

Her lips pressed together for a moment before she answered. "I think that if I don't make a huge statement like that, I won't last a semester before I'm back home."

Gently, I took my hands away from her. "I still don't see what's so bad about that."

She shrugged, slowly and helplessly. "I can't explain it any better, Darce. Just... It's what I want. What I think I need. You don't have to be happy about it, but stop punishing me. Please? I'll be gone soon enough."

I sighed. "I'm not trying to punish you."

"Then can we stop this?" She waved an arm, encompassing the air between us. "Please?"

"Yeah. Sure. We can stop fighting."

But I left without hugging her and I ate lunch by myself.

121

It was weight day, so I knew Jean would be hitting the gym after school. But not fighting and having the heart to act like nothing was wrong were different things, so I hit the track on the other side of town instead.

Two miles into my run, someone came up behind me and hovered there for half a lap before pulling beside me. I wasn't sure who I expected it to be, but Adam wasn't it. Despite Jean's obsession, I'd never had too much to do with him. Not when other people weren't around, anyway. Weird that he'd want to talk to me now, when I was sweaty and my hair was all over the place, rather than when I didn't look like and smell like a monster.

"Hey," he grunted. "How's it going?"

"Fine," I said. I didn't say anything else, hoping he'd think I was conserving breath rather than being rude. In reality, I just didn't have a clue what I was supposed to talk about.

"So, Lucas said I should take Jean to the dance."

I nodded, although I was a little confused. Lucas hadn't just told Jean what was going on, but had actually set her up with Adam? No wondered she'd jumped up and hugged him. He had to be a lot higher on her list of favorite people right then than I was.

"You do everything he says?" I asked. I should have been happy for Jean, I knew that. But mostly I was annoyed. It didn't seem fair that the guy who'd kept me from helping was the one hooking Jean and Adam up now. Why should he get credit for something he'd tried to stop?

Adam laughed. "If I can. He's a lot smarter than me."

Huh. Likely true, though a little bit scary.

"He saw how special she was before I did," Adam went on. "Said she was too good for me."

My foot hit wrong and I stumbled a little as I tried to save my balance. It probably looked funny, but at least I didn't face plant. What Adam had just said was an awful lot like what Lucas told me back in that assembly about how Jean deserved better. "What changed his mind?"

"Don't know." Adam shrugged, not looking too concerned.

122

"Something. He all but ordered me to take her to the Waltz. Not that I didn't want to ask her already. I was just worried what he'd say, you know?"

"Right." I nodded, having to force myself to watch the track instead of staring at Adam.

"Honestly, I thought he wanted to take her himself."

I nearly tripped again, although it wasn't that radical a thought. It had certainly occurred to me that Lucas was interested in Jean. She was tall and blonde and didn't argue with him like I did. He'd be stupid not to like her, right?

"But I guess not," Adam said. "Or he would have."

I wasn't so sure, because he'd seen my argument with her and knew how much Jean wanted to be with Adam. He'd have known she'd say no if he asked her. Could he possibly like her enough to set her up with someone else just to see her happy? Or maybe he wanted on her good side so that when it didn't work out with Adam, he'd be able to step in?

I veered off the track as we approached the bench where I'd left my stuff. "Need a drink."

"Okay, sure."

I expected him to say that it had been great seeing me and keep going, but he stopped when I did and followed me over. He locked an arm behind his head and stretched as I grabbed my water bottle. A pair of women jogged by on the track, one of them nearly colliding with the other as she craned her neck to watch him. It would have made Hunter grin, but Adam didn't even notice.

"So, what about you?" he asked, switching arms to stretch. "You have plans for the dance?"

Lowering the bottle, I shook my head. "No. I hate dances."

"Okay. That's what Jean said. I just wanted to be sure."

"Um... Thanks." I took another drink, wondering what he would have done if I'd told him I was heartbroken not to be going.

"If you change your mind, let me know."

I snapped the plug down on the bottle. "If I change my mind, I'll go buy a dress and you'll see me there."

His lips curved up. He really did have a nice smile. "Alright."

I tossed the bottle back on my jacket and we ran another mile.

FROM: hstgeorge@catskill.edu
TO: darcybennet@merytonhs.com
SUBJECT: Questions

I'd love to tell myself you're not getting my texts, but I know you're just ignoring them. That's pretty passive-aggressive, you know. You could at least tell me to leave you alone.

But I think I know why you're ignoring me and I guess it's my fault. It's because I didn't want to talk about Ellen, isn't it? Well, I still don't, but if you're not going to talk to me unless I do, here goes.

I moved to Meryton in June to fix up the house my aunt had just bought. In exchange, I get to stay in the apartment over her garage instead of a dorm and had the satisfaction of bossing my cousin around all summer.

One of the first things I did was look up the curling club. It was closed, of course, but I met Ellen in the office. And we went out for a few weeks, until I realized the bitch is bat-shit crazy.

In the interest of full honesty, that's not the end of the story. There have been a few times when she's forgotten we broke up and on a couple of them I've taken more advantage of it than I should have. Which probably makes you think I'm an asshole, but hopefully I'll at least get points for being an honest asshole.

I like you, Darcy. A lot more than I ever liked her. Answer my texts?

Peace and Love,

Hunter

Chapter Eighteen

Friday night, I laid on my bed with my favorite band blaring on the stereo as I stared at the bumps on my ceiling. The song was about how everyone leaves. Yeah, I could relate.

There was a bang on my door and then Mom stuck her head in. "You're nowhere near ready!"

Ready? She must have meant that I wasn't packed for the trip that most of the family was taking over the weekend. Kevin was staying home because of hockey. I was staying to curl. There'd been a big discussion about how we couldn't miss our stuff but Shel and the twins couldn't miss his mom's birthday. Mom hadn't wanted to leave us alone, but Shel convinced her we'd be fine. "I'm not going with you. Curling tournament, remember?"

Sure, she had a lot going on with work and the twins and having to visit her mother-in-law, but it hurt that she'd completely forgotten the tournament she'd be missing.

She came into the room and turned down the volume of my music. "I know that, honey. But aren't you going to the dance tonight?"

I propped myself up on my elbows and stared at her. "In three and a half years, I have yet to go to a school dance. What makes you think I'd start now?"

"I thought you had a date."

I shook my head. We'd gone over this. "Someone asked me, but I didn't want to go."

126

"Didn't want to go?" The bed dipped as she sat down next to me. "Or didn't want to go with him?"

"Mom..." I rolled my eyes. "It's the twenty-first century. If I wanted to go with someone else, I would've asked someone else."

"Okay..." She reached out and brushed my hair back, like she thought I needed comforting. "If you're sure, honey."

"Yo, sis!" Kevin called from the hall before walking in to join the party. Why did I even have a doorway? No one respected it as a barrier. "Where are your keys?"

"Her keys?" Mom asked.

I ignored our mother. "For my brother, you're looking pretty good, Kev."

He grinned. "You don't have to flatter me, you're the one doing me a favor."

"Doh! I got that backwards, huh?" I played along, but I'd meant what I said. Baby bro cleaned up well. Lisa had messed up saying no when he asked her to the dance, and the girl who'd said yes would be thrilled to see him. I pointed at my dresser. "They're up there. Try not to hit anything, k? I need it early tomorrow."

He snatched them up. "No promises."

"Kevin..." Mom said slowly.

He rolled his eyes. "I won't hit anything. Or speed. Or make turns without signaling. I do know how to drive. Got my license and everything."

"Two weeks ago," Mom said.

"Which means it's still fresh in my mind." Kev tapped his temple with a wicked smile that made me laugh.

I moved around Mom to give him a hug. I had to go up on my toes to whisper in his ear. My toes! When had he gotten so tall? "Good luck."

"Thanks," he whispered back. "And thanks for the car. I owe you."

I stood back and nodded. "Yep. Don't go forgetting it either."

Mom nibbled her lip as she watched us, but she gave Kevin a smile before he left. "Home by midnight, kiddo. Have fun."

He waved over his shoulder as he left the room.

Mom turned and looked at me. "So, you're really okay about the dance?"

"Yes, Mom." Sheesh. "Why wouldn't I be?"

She shrugged. "I don't know. But something's wrong. If it's not that, what is it?"

"Nothing."

She gave me a long, narrow look.

With an aggravated grunt, I leaned against my dresser, then folded my arms and picked at the cuff of my sleeve. "Jean's going to the University of California."

"California." Mom winced. "That's far."

"Yeah. Tell me about it."

"How about you?" She watched me closely, looking a little scared. Did she think I'd run away to the West Coast too?

"I'm not going anywhere," I said, dropping my eyes to the carpet. "I'm too boring to want to leave."

"You're not boring, honey. And Jean doesn't think that either."

My shoulders trembled as I shook my head. "She says she can't stand staying here. She needs to escape. What does that say about me?"

"Nothing." Mom got off the bed and took a few steps toward me. "Does it say anything about Jean that you want to stay here instead of going with her? Or does it just mean that you've found your place in the world and she's still looking?"

I frowned and thought about that. I hadn't really tried turning the accusations around. Occasionally Mom can be freakishly smart.

Mom kissed the top of my bent head. "Jean loves you. Her leaving doesn't change that any more than your staying does."

She closed the door behind her with a quiet click.

For about an hour, I just stared at the ceiling and pondered until I was nearly crazy from it. Hoping a walk would help clear my thoughts, I grabbed my headphones and headed outside. It was cold enough that I took my ski jacket, but the icy air caressing my cheeks was just what I needed. Somehow, cold always made me feel better.

How could Jean stand the thought of leaving this? Of going somewhere with no weather? How could she not run in fear from the idea of it being summer all the time? I still didn't know, but Mom had helped me put it in perspective.

Jean wasn't me.

I'd always known that, of course, but I guess I'd been caught up in the similarities.

Without thinking about it, I walked to the curling club. The building was dark, dead. But inside, the ice was alive and well. Better than usual, because they'd closed down the second half of the week to get the surfaces ready for the bonspiels. First the juniors, then the adult Yule Spiel the following weekend.

Petre's wasn't much more active. The over-twenty-one crowd had other places to go on Fridays and the high schoolers were all at the dance. Except for me. I examined my feelings about that, like poking your tongue at a missing tooth, but I honestly wasn't upset about it. Dances weren't my thing. I didn't know when they'd become Jean's. Maybe they always had been but she'd never said anything before.

Once I stopped moving, the cold started seeping into me and I decided after a few minutes to drift into the pizzeria for some cocoa and a round of pinball.

One game of pinball turned into three, which turned into five dollars worth.

Something about the pinball helped ease me the rest of the way out of my Jean-funk. Everything would be okay. I'd survive her crossing the country. Our friendship would survive it. Heck, she might not even go if things worked out well enough with Adam. Rumor had it he was in line for a hockey scholarship at Catskill.

I took out my phone to send her a text saying how sorry I was for being so immature lately and asking how things were going with Adam, but it beeped with my message tone just before I got it open. I started to smile. It was just like things used to be, with us reading each other's minds even from across town.

129

The smile died when I flicked the phone open and saw who the message was from. Not Jean, but Lisa. "Need help. Don't tell Jean."

Help? That wasn't too vague or anything. Not likely to make me panic at all. I clicked out my response as fast as I could. "What kind of help?"

I stood there staring at the phone. And staring. And staring. The seconds ticked by and no new message came in.

I dialed her number. Voice mail. "Shit, Lisa! What do you mean, you need help? Help with your makeup? Help finding your keys? Help escaping a serial killer? God! Text me!"

Hanging up, I took several deep breaths. No call. No new text.

It was probably something harmless. Probably. Except why couldn't I tell Jean?

Shoving my coat back on, I went outside. Clouds had come in to cover the moon, making it darker than when I'd gone in. The air was crisper too, filled with a promise of imminent snow.

I started walking toward the school. As far as I knew, Lisa went to the dance, just not with my brother. She probably wanted help breaking into one of the classrooms or something.

The phone beeped and I nearly dropped it in my eagerness to get it out of my pocket. Another text from Lisa! "On train to Poughkeepsie. Need ride home. Broke. Alone. Help? (Don't tell Jean!)"

Poughkeepsie? I yanked my gloves off to type back. "Did you go to the city?"

I walked as I waited for a response and I made it to the school without getting one. If she was in Manhattan, she might have gone underground and lost coverage. I sent a second message. "I'll be there. Don't know when. What's your ETA?"

My car wasn't in the parking lot. Crap. I sent a text to Kevin. "Emergency! Need car! Where are you?"

Then I sent another message, this time to Hunter. "What are you up to?"

The phone beeped almost instantly, Hunter getting back to

me before anyone else. "In Brooklyn with my cousin. Don't worry, I'll be back for first draw tomorrow!"

Ugh. Not the answer I'd hoped for. It was late enough that Lisa was likely on the last train out of the city. Even if Hunter had left his car at our end of the line, it wouldn't do us any good.

I put my gloves back on and tried to think. I could see why Lisa didn't want Jean to know she was in trouble. Much as I loved Jean, she'd always been a snitch. Telling Lisa was the same as telling any of our parents. And the last thing we wanted was Lisa grounded during the bonspiel.

I corrected that thought quickly. The last thing we wanted was Lisa assaulted, raped, or murdered. Or even spending the night huddled scared at a train station.

Poughkeepsie was far enough away that she wasn't going to be able to get a cab without money upfront unless she was lucky enough to find a cabbie who moonlighted as a saint.

I might have to tattle. Grounded was better than dead.

A group of people came out of the building, but I was too busy thinking to pay any attention to them until one of the figures split off and walked my way. With all the negative thoughts in my head, it would have been natural for that to worry me, but I recognized the lope even before I could see him clearly. Lucas.

Not my first choice for a white knight and probably not Lisa's either. But I'd seen the way he looked at his niece, and I could use that devotion to get him to help someone else's little girl.

"Hey." He stopped a few feet away and frowned at me as he took in the details of my expression. He was wearing a dark burgundy shirt with a chestnut tie. It was more fall than winter, but it looked good on him. "You okay?"

"Yes. No." I took a breath. This wasn't going quite right.

"Do you want me to get Jean?" He glanced behind him. "She's still here."

"No!"

He looked back slowly. "You're kind of scaring me, Darcy."

131

Really? Maybe I wasn't holding onto my panic as well as I'd hoped. "Jean can't know. Lisa's on a train to Poughkeepsie."

"Poughkeepsie?"

"Yeah, Poughkeepsie." I struggled not to hyperventilate. "I don't know what happened, just that she texted me and said she needed help. And we can't tell Jean because she'd tell their mom. But I lent my car to Kevin and he's gone already and he won't answer my texts and I don't think he went home, but maybe he did..."

I turned and started walking before I'd finished the sentence, but I only got about a yard before Lucas grabbed my arm. "You can't drive like this."

"Not until I find my car, no."

He grunted. "Especially not if you find your car."

"What?" I looked up at him and tried to focus. He looked nice. Really nice. I shook my head. He was right, I was in no shape to drive anywhere until I calmed down some.

"Stay here," he said. He gave me a long look before he trotted a little way off to say something to the people he'd been with. He waved at them as he came back to me. "You got any money?"

Um... "About twenty bucks."

"Good." He took keys from his pocket, tossed them a foot into the air, and caught them again. "We'll need gas."

Chapter Nineteen

We stopped at the gas station on the edge of town, and combing my pockets, I managed to gather enough cash to fund twenty dollars in gas and coffee for each of us. Drip. Black. Lucas smiled when I gave him his and settled beside him to watch the numbers creep up on the pump.

My pocket chimed and I grabbed my phone quickly, hoping it was good news from Lisa. It wasn't. It was a picture from Colin of him and Scarlet cuddling together at a table decorated with way too much crepe paper. Scarlet looked cute, but Colin... Well, I dodged a bullet there.

"Wow," Lucas breathed over my shoulder, a hint of laughter in the single word.

"Yeah," I agreed as I went to delete the picture.

I paused before erasing though, my attention caught on a detail in the background. Was that Jean? I could only see a sliver of the girl's side, but the hair looked like hers.

Lucas pulled his phone out of his coat. "I have a better picture of Jean."

"You do?"

The wind ruffled his hair as he scrolled through pictures in his photo gallery. "Yeah. I got a couple of her. This is the best one, I think."

He held it up for me to see. It was a good picture. The lighting fell perfectly on her wide smile and the shadows behind her brought out the shimmering texture of her long silver dress. She looked gorgeous. And really, really happy.

Unshed tears stung my eyes as I shook my head in response to Lucas gesturing that I could take the phone. I swallowed my ridiculous emotions and got in the car while he closed the gas cap. The car was well-used, but mostly clean. A lot like my car aside from the fact that this was a stick and mine was an automatic. It was an older Subaru, from back when the Outback looked more like a station wagon and less like a small SUV. Not stylish, but great on snow. Which was good because flakes were drifting lazily down by the time we finished fueling up.

It was dark. It was cold. I couldn't go more than five minutes without texting Lisa, which I could tell was driving her nuts. But... The seats had warmers and mine worked, although Lucas said the driver's side had burned out years ago, back when the car was still his dad's. The snow was pretty. And Lucas let me hook my phone into the sound system instead of insisting we listen to his music. Although maybe I would have turned out to like his music. He knew and seemed to like most of mine.

We didn't talk much. None of the questions I could think to ask him seemed like things I had the right to know. Why did he quit curling? What did his sister die of? He'd told me his niece lived with them. But where was her father?

"It was a car accident," he said somewhere on the outskirts of Poughkeepsie.

"What?" I frowned at his profile. His skin glowed an odd blueish color in the light of the speedometer and both of his hands gripped the steering wheel. Ten and two. Just like the driver's ed books said.

"You want to know how Michelle died, but you don't want to ask." He tried to smile. "I recognize the expression."

"Oh." I shifted awkwardly. "I'm sorry. Car accident, huh?"

"Yeah."

I looked out the front window as the car raced into the night.

"No," he said, although I hadn't asked anything. "No

134

alcohol. No drugs. Bright, sunny day... Michelle died instantly. Amelia was touch and go for a while."

My stomach twisted. "Oh, God. That poor kid."

He shrugged like it was nothing much, but even in the dark I could see how tense his entire body was. I wanted to reach out and touch him. Squeeze his shoulder. Hold his hand... But his hand stayed on the wheel and I couldn't quite bring myself to invade his grief. "For about a year, I was the only one she'd talk to."

He gave a shudder suddenly, shaking his head and straightening in his seat.

We fell silent for a few minutes. I tried to listen to the music, but I was hyper-focused on Lucas. "You know, I think it's great that you're so close to her. It's sweet. I mean, Kevin hardly knows the twins are alive. But Amelia... She's lucky to have you."

His throat cleared a few times. "Um... Thanks. Guess there's one thing you like about me then."

One.... I twisted until I could look straight at his profile. We were in town now and there was plenty of light to show me his expression. It didn't do much good. Even in full detail, I didn't know what his expression meant. Nerves? Anger? Embarrassment?

"There's also your heated car seats," I said, attempting levity.

He chuckled. "Car seat. Singular."

"Right. My bad."

We turned into the train station and he pulled into the loading zone. Inside the building, a figure that looked like Lisa was waiting, but I didn't text her immediately. "Lucas?"

He took a long breath and turned his head toward me. "Yeah?"

His jaw was tight, but his eyes... They were soft, vulnerable. Maybe a little hurt.

"Thank you for doing this."

A flicker of a smile. "No problem. I'm not really an after party kind of guy anyway."

135

Biting down hard on the inside of my lip, I dropped my eyes and pulled my phone out. I flipped it open, but I still didn't type. My hands shook too much for me to type. "I like that about you too."

"Yeah?" The word was a whisper. Or maybe a prayer.

The back door opened and I let out a little shriek. The phone fell to the floorboard with a thump, disconnecting the music and plunging the car into silence for half a second before Lisa's laughter kicked in.

"Hey, guys," she said brightly. "Thanks for the ride!"

Thanks for the ride? How about thanks for driving two hours from home in the middle of a snowy night on no notice?

Her door still wide open, she turned behind her. "Hey, guys! My ride's here!"

A group of guys dressed in J Crew and all holding open bottles of beer made a collective groan. One of them broke apart to approach us. "You don't have to go, baby. You can party with us."

I glanced at Lucas. He shrugged, completely out of his element. I pushed a button to lower my window and leaned out. The stench of stale cigarette smoke weaved through the cold air. I was kind of relieved it was a tobacco scent and not something less legal. "Thanks for taking care of my friend, guys. She's only fifteen and kind of stupid."

Their eyes widened and a couple of them actually took a few awkward steps backward.. The one who'd been chasing Lisa stopped and gaped at her for a second. She was dressed for clubbing, perching on three inch heels, and wearing half a cosmetics rack on her face. To me it screamed of trying too hard, which made her seem at least as young as she was. But these guys were obviously drunk and seemed to have thought she was older.

She laughed, not at all offended by what I'd said. "Don't mind her, she's a prude. But thanks for keeping me company. I'll call you next time I'm in town."

There were a few cat calls of encouragement, like they'd already forgotten the part about her being severely underage.

136

The lead drunk guy reached out toward Lisa, but she evaded him easily and finally got into the car.

The second Lisa shut her door, Lucas started the car back into motion, getting us out of there before the frat rejects could decide they didn't want Lisa leaving after all, or worse, tried to stop us.

We pulled back onto the road home and Lucas looked up into the rear view mirror. Lisa was babbling out a story about some hipster on the train talking about his deadbeat brother. "So, Lisa, why did you go into the city in the first place?"

He asked it like he didn't really care and was just being polite. But he interrupted her mid-sentence to ask.

"Oh," she switched track without stumbling. "Hunter."

"Hunter?" I asked, twisting to gawk at her. "Hunter's in Brooklyn."

She rolled her eyes. "Yeah, well he went into Manhattan tonight."

"And he invited you?"

"Yes." She gave me a square look. "And you have no right being jealous. I saw him before you did."

"Saw him?" I squeaked. With a growl, I folded my arms and swiveled to face forward. I wasn't jealous, but I was angry. What the hell was Hunter thinking taking someone like Lisa into the city? And then leaving her there!

Lucas cleared his throat. "So, to clarify... Your teammate's boyfriend took you into Manhattan and ditched you there?"

Lisa snorted. "He's not her boyfriend. Not outside her dreams."

"Oh?" Lucas stared at her in the rear view and something stabbed through my heart, telling me that I needed to stop him before he said whatever he was about to say.

"Of course he isn't," I said quickly.

The stare moved to me. "Kinda looked like it in the parking lot."

"What?" Lisa shrieked.

"Gee, thanks," I muttered.

Lucas turned his eyes back to the road as his cheeks flamed

137

red. "Shouldn't do secret things in public."

"What?" Lisa repeated. She slammed her hand into the back of my seat. "What were you doing in the parking lot?"

"Nothing," I murmured.

"Lucas?" Lisa stuck her head through the seats, bringing her mouth close to his ear. "What did you see?"

He shrugged. "Nothing."

"Nothing?" she repeated, sliding closer. My teeth grit together as she brought her hand up and ran it along his arm. "Nothing at all?"

He glanced her way, his expression annoyed. "Nothing."

She smacked him and the car veered into the oncoming lane.

"Fucking hell!" Lucas screamed. He turned enough to shove Lisa away. "Get your damn seat belt on!"

As Lisa tumbled back, her mouth open and her eyes swimming with tears, Lucas turned back to driving. His breaths were jagged and his fingers gripped the wheel so tight I was almost scared he'd break it.

With a jerk, he yanked the car over in the next parking lot. It was fast food place, still open even though it was after midnight. He got out without saying anything, leaving the keys in the ignition.

I stared at the keys for a few minutes as Lisa sobbed quietly in the back.

"His sister died in a car accident," I said after awhile.

"So?" Lisa sniffled.

I shook my head, grabbed the keys, and got out of the car.

I went in just as Lucas came out of the bathroom.

"Hey," he said, looking at his shoes. Despite the dress slacks and tie, he had on his usual pair of well-loved high-tops. I hadn't noticed them before and they made me smile a little. Part of me felt I should be mad at him for blabbing about me and Hunter, but my anger over that had flown out the window the second Lisa made us cross the double yellow line.

"Hey," I said, keeping my voice gentle. "You want anything?"

He shrugged. "Could go for coffee."

"Me too." I widened my smile. "You got any money?"

That got him to laugh, though he didn't sound too mirthful. "We should make Princess Jail Bait pay for it."

I snickered at the title. Normally I'd defend her, but I was tired and she was being a royal brat. "Yeah, but then we'd have to go talk to her."

"Good point."

He stepped up to the counter, telling the bored-looking woman there that we wanted two coffees. We drank them in the restaurant, sitting across from each other in a comfortable silence.

TO: hstgeorge@catskill.edu
FROM: darcybennet@merytonhs.com
SUBJECT: WTF?

So, do you know why I texted you? Can you guess?

Here's a clue... Underage girl abandoned in Manhattan.

Yeah, that's right. Lisa called me in to rescue her after you lured her into the city and then ditched her without a way home.

What the hell were you thinking? What's wrong with you? Are you aware she's fifteen? FIFTEEN! And she's from Meryton, which doesn't exactly breed street smarts into people.

Do you have any idea what kinds of things could happen to a cute fifteen-year-old alone and clueless? She didn't even have money for the train to Poughkeepsie -- she had to beg someone to buy her a ticket! And then beg me to come get her there.

You can't treat people like that. And you damned sure can't treat my teammates like that.

- Darcy

Chapter Twenty

Grains of sleep still stuck to my eyes as I staggered into the curling club the next morning. To my astonishment, both Lisa and Lucas had beaten me in. They were huddled together with cups of coffee bought from the little stand sat up in the corner. It was meant for the spectators, not for those of us playing first draw, but I couldn't fault Lisa for the pre-game caffeine intake when I was so tired I could hardly stand.

But why was Lucas there?

Lisa's hand went to his arm as she laughed about something. Apparently Lucas coming to her rescue had combined with Hunter's abandonment in the city to shift her crush. Maybe that had something to do with Lucas being around.

I'd been thinking that maybe I wanted some coffee too, but I turned away and went into the locker room. When I came back out, Cat had joined Lisa and was waving her hands around dramatically. Lisa's eyes were huge, panicked.

I crossed the room quickly, weaving through the gathering crowd. "What's wrong? Is Maria okay?"

"Scheduling conflict," Lucas said. His arms were folded tightly and he shook his head a lot. There were deep circles under his eyes, making his unhappy expression darker and more intense.

"What do you mean?"

He looked to Cat, who answered in a higher pitch than

usual. "Maria has SAT's."

"SAT's?" I repeated, dumbfounded.

Lisa made a funny, angry, little grunt. "And she didn't tell us! Can you believe it?"

"Wait..." I was still trying to wrap my sleepy brain around what was happening. "You guys are saying our second simply isn't here? Because she's taking a standardized test?"

"One that's she's known about for ages!" Lisa continued. For someone who'd run off into the city the night before, she embraced her outrage with remarkable fervor.

Lucas gave his head another shake. "And she sent her girlfriend to break the news."

My eyes snapped to him, glaring. Maria's actions were cowardly alright, but where did he get off dissing my teammate?

There was a laugh behind me. "Yeah," said Hunter. "When you walked out on our team, at least you announced it in person."

I spun around, my anger jumping from Lucas to Hunter. "You stay the hell out of this. Way the hell out of this. Other side of the room out of this."

He smiled at me. The snake! "Good morning to you too."

My fingers wrung the handle of my broom. If I wasn't careful, I'd wind up snapping it in two. Then I'd be out two hundred dollars on top of everything else.

I took a deep breath and looked back to the others. "It's okay. You up for subbing, Cat?"

"Me?" She paled at the thought, but nodded. She played in a noncompetitive league with her family, so she knew the game, though she didn't play as seriously as we did.

"Great. You two decide who's playing lead and who's second, then I'll let the organizers know."

Hunter's hand landed on my shoulder and I froze. "I love a girl who can take charge."

I hit him. Took my broom in both hands and slammed the handle lengthwise into his chest. "I do not want to talk to you."

"Whoa!" His hands went up defensively, but he laughed like

142

he didn't think I was a threat. We'd see who was laughing when I got the broom up his ass!

Swiftly, Lucas wrapped a hand around my arm, his grip just firm enough to get my attention. I snapped my head to see him watching me with a understanding glint in his eye. "Not that I don't want to see you tear him apart, but you may have another problem."

"Like what?" Hunter asked. My estimate of his IQ was dropping by the instant. Why wasn't he leaving?

Lucas glanced around the room. "No one's seen Jean."

"Since when?" I asked, looking at Lisa. "She didn't bring you in?"

My teammate shook her head. "No, I called Lucas. Jean's car wasn't at home. I... Well, I assumed she was still with Adam. But neither of them will answer their phones."

I yanked my arm free of Lucas and stalked around Hunter to survey the room. Lots of people I knew, more than I would have expected at the hour. But no Jean. She hadn't been in the locker room when I was there and she would have had to walk past us to be there now. "Upstairs?"

"I didn't see her," Lucas said, but he and Hunter followed me when I went to check.

Nope. She wasn't hanging in the rec area. Not in the kitchen. No sign of her in the bathroom. Where was she then?

I took out my phone. We still had five minutes before taking the ice, but she never cut it that close. I sent a quick message as I walked back down the stairs. "Where are you?"

I stopped near the door and stared at my phone, willing it to do something. She had to be safe. She was just with Adam. And if she'd been with him all night... Well, you didn't have to be a genius to figure out why maybe she hadn't woken up on time.

Hunter inched way too close to me. He smelled like the cologne that Lucas used to wear. Who puts on cologne to play sports? Especially cologne that gross. "Maybe you should call her?"

"Maybe you should go to Hell."

143

Lucas drifted off toward the organizers as I glared at my phone, which still refused to show any new messages.

"Are you mad at me?" Hunter asked.

"Am I mad at you?" I stared up at him. "I'm freaking pissed at you. How could you do that to Lisa?"

He frowned, confused. "Do what to Lisa?"

He looked back to where we'd left her. She was pointing out our opponents to Cat, and if she worried at all about her sister, she did a good job of hiding it.

"Do what?" I repeated. Was he serious?

His eyes shifted from wide and confused to narrowed and angry. "Stop playing parrot and tell me what I did."

"You lured her into the city and then left her there!"

He laughed. Laughed!

"And now you're laughing about it?" I shoved past him, heading toward the organizers.

His hand lashed out to grab me. "Lured? Darcy, I didn't lure anyone. I'm not even sure I know how to lure."

I yanked my arm free but didn't start walking again. He met my eyes easily, but I wasn't sure he was being honest. "One of you is lying."

He shrugged. "I told her I was going to see my cousin's band play a gig in the village. I didn't say anything about her coming."

It didn't take much imagination to see how Lisa could have construed being told about the trip to being invited along. Still... How many details had he given her? She'd known enough to know where she was heading or she wouldn't have left home. And why give her that much information if she wasn't invited?

Lucas came back, his shoulders sloped and his whole face frowning. Stephanie was with him and she looked even less pleased. "Where are Maria and Lisa?"

"Lisa's over there." I pointed across the room, the motion capturing Lisa's attention. I waved her over. "Maria isn't here."

Steph frowned even harder than she already was. "Where is she then? You told me on the phone you girls had worked everything out."

I took a deep breath. "She's retaking the SAT's. Cat's playing instead."

"Oh." She shook her head. "Well, Cat's good.... But I don't know if you're going to be playing anyway."

"What do you mean?"

Hunter put a hand on my shoulder. "Breathe, Darcy. What's up, Steph? You know where Jean is?"

She nodded, but waited for Lisa to make it to us before she said anything. "Girls, this is hard to tell you..."

My knees started to weaken and I looked to Lucas, trying to see how dire his expression was. He gave me a tiny smile. So the news wasn't going to be good, but it wasn't as bad as it could be.

Steph took a deep breath. "Jean's been arrested. She's in jail."

"What?" I blurted, the word loud enough to carry into the room and make heads turn to me. "Jail? Why? What happened? Are you sure?"

Hunter's fingers rubbed against my tense muscles, but rather than relaxing me, it made me more jittery.

"Is she okay?" Lisa asked. Her eyes were as wide as they could go. Under other circumstances the look would have been comical.

"Yeah, she's fine." Stephanie pinched the bridge of her nose. "Just stupid. I don't have details, but I don't think she's being charged with anything. She was just taken into custody at some party she went to last night. She'll be released soon, but your mom's not letting her come."

And I knew her mom too well to think there was a chance at an appeal. The former Mrs. Smith had been curling at our club since she was tiny, but it wouldn't make a difference. She knew the punishment screwed all of us, but she'd figure that would make it more effective.

My eyes cast around the room and I tried not to whimper out loud over the fact that I didn't see anyone who was a.) female b.) young enough for Juniors and c.) not already in the tournament. Any second they'd start the welcome announcements, and as soon as those where over, we'd be expected to either take the ice or drop out.

Lucas nodded to himself. "I'll get Maria."

He turned and left, making it to the door before I shook off Hunter's hand and ran after him. I slammed to a stop on the threshold, realizing at the last second that I had my game shoes on. "Lucas!"

He stopped and turned, looking at me expectantly. And a bit impatiently.

"We should try calling her."

He waited, shifting from foot to foot like he needed to pee. The phone didn't even ring before going to voice mail.

"Ugh. Her phone's off."

He nodded. "Testing center wouldn't let it be on. I'll handle it."

I slid my phone in my pocket. "Are you sure?"

A smile flickered over his face. "Trust me."

From THE CATSKILL CURLING CLUB HANDBOOK

In some situations, a team may find it necessary to play with only three players. In this situation, the first and second players will both throw three rocks rather than the customary two.

Note that you will also be limited to one sweeper unless the delivering player can sweep his own rock. For this reason, we recommend finding a substitute if at all possible should the absent member be expected to miss a significant amount of play.

A fourth player may enter the game between ends, at which point the game will proceed as normal.

Chapter Twenty-One

We had a choice, we could either play with three people or we could give up points and possibly the entire game as a delay penalty. Thirty minutes without Maria would have cost us two ends and two points. Thirty one minutes would cost the game. We had no idea how long Lucas would take to get her.

We started without a fourth player, which isn't a lot of fun. It means most players throw extra rocks and there's only one available sweeper, who has to work overtime and wears out in a flash.

We passed the thirty minute mark without any sign of Maria.

At forty minutes after start time, just before my last throw of the third end, Maria showed up, flushed and breathing fast. Her dreads were down instead of tied up like usual and she was in jeans, not her usual athletic gear, but I'd never been happier to see her.

I hugged her as soon as she got close enough. "About time my vice-skip got here!"

"I'm sorry," she said. Her eyes went to the scoreboard and she winced. "We yellow?"

"Afraid so."

She groaned. "God, I'm really sorry."

"It's okay. You didn't know Jean wouldn't be here."

Down the ice, Cat held the broom where I'd told her I wanted to aim and waved with her free hand.

"Good to see you," Lisa said. "Let's curl, Darcy!"

Maria stood back as I went into the hack and threw. The rock left my hand feeling perfect and glided to exactly the right spot. It clunked into one red stone, then another. The second red rock hit a third. Triple take-out, baby!

The opposing skip whistled. "Beautiful shot."

I grinned at her. "Just trying to give you a challenge so you don't feel like you didn't get to play."

She laughed. "Thanks."

Despite the awesome shot, our zen was way off and we closed the match with a loss. It was a close loss though, which almost felt like a win considering how poorly we started.

We had the next draw off and we were all glad of it. The others went to find food while I opted for a nap in the backseat of my car. It was cold and the sun was bright, but I was wiped enough to be asleep in minutes.

When my phone chirped to wake me up a few hours later, I was under a plush blanket that hadn't been there before. I drew it to my nose, breathing in like I thought I could smell the person who'd put it there. But, it didn't smell like anyone in particular so much as it smelled like fabric softener. Lavender. The graphics were a little more of a clue.

I folded the blanket, smiling at the Disney princesses on it, and took it in the building to find its owner. She was by the glass upstairs, bouncing up and down in excitement over the game she was watching. Her pigtails waved around like little arms.

"Hey, Amelia."

She glanced at me long enough to see the blanket but then looked back at the ice. "I think my cousin's losing."

"Your cousin?"

She nodded. "Hunter."

"Hunter's your cousin?"

She sighed in exasperation and took the blanket from me. "Duh."

"Oh." Duh? They don't have the same name. They don't look alike. Why was I supposed to think Amelia and Hunter were related... "Wait, if he's your cousin, what is he to Lucas?"

"His cousin." She shook her head as Hunter's opponent landed a shot that seriously messed with the odds of a steal. That was bad news for Team Saint George because Amelia was right about them loosing. They were down one and this was last end, so they needed to score. "Hunter and Lucas have the same grandparents. That's how cousins work."

Wow, no one can call you an idiot like a six-year-old.

"Right."

We were quiet as Hunter lined up for his last shot, our breaths held.

"Aim's good," I said.

It landed perfectly, sliding between two guards and curling around the opponent's stone to land right on the button. Not only was it shot rock, but it was well protected. Hunter would have the point unless his opponents pulled off something seriously brilliant.

Nearby, a middle-aged woman bearing a strong resemblance to Hunter jumped up and started cheering, as if he could hear her through all the glass. She was wearing a sweater covered in curling rocks and dangling earrings that looked like sheets of curling ice.

"That's Penelope," Amelia said. "She's my grandma. Lucas's mother. Hunter's aunt."

If my brothers had spelled it out to that degree, I would have smacked them. I don't hit other people's kids though, so Amelia was safe from popping. "Thanks for the blanket."

She shrugged. "It was Lucas. You should thank him."

Um... "Okay."

"He's over there." She turned and pointed to the back of the room. Thankfully, Lucas didn't notice because he was facing the other way, bent over a table painted in concentric circles to look like a house. My teammates studied whatever he was doing, Lisa from about an inch away from him. No, less than an inch. As I was watching, she put her hand on his shoulder, like she needed the support to stay balanced as she looked at the table.

150

My teeth were clenched together as I moved my attention back to Hunter's game.

His opponent took his time choosing a shot, finally calling a risky move that would either win the game or lose it.

As his rock left his hand, it looked good. Maybe a little hard, but it should have been alright. The sweepers though... What were they thinking? They swept the whole way. Stupid mistake.

The stone smacked into a guard. That was fine. It was supposed to hit the guard and let it roll into the house. But it hit with way too much force and the guard sailed into a third rock. All three of them stopped well outside Hunter's closest rocks.

Penelope started cheering again and Amelia cleared her throat. "You should thank people when they do nice things. It's polite."

It took me a second to figure out what she meant because I was still thinking about that last shot, wondering if I would have been able to make it.

"Lucas," she said. "He was nice to you."

Good grief. Like Lucas needed me thanking him. Surely Lisa had thanked him enough already.

As I walked over anyway, he shifted away from her, putting a chair between them before he reached down to move a coaster. I suspected he could have moved it from where he was before, but I wasn't sure what to make of that. Did he not want Lisa draped over him? Because most guys wouldn't have a problem with it.

He smiled at me as I got closer and then moved a second coaster.

"What do you think?" he asked me. "You're the right-side-up coasters."

I took a new coaster from the stack on the edge of the table as I studied the layout. "In through here. Land like this."

Lucas grinned as I put the coaster down and Lisa made an annoyed sound. "He said you'd say that. You were supposed to back me up."

151

"Sorry." I shrugged. "What did you want to do?"

She moved the coaster to a spot that would be great except there's no way the rock could get there.

"Impossible," I said. I touched two of the opposing coasters. "There's not enough space between these. You'd hit one of them."

She stared at the table, then hit Lucas's arm with the back of her hand. "Why didn't you say that? What was all that babbling about angles and arcs?"

Maria laughed. "Same thing."

"No, it isn't!" Lisa insisted, picking up the coasters.

"So..." Lucas jerked his head toward where his mom was still acting like a madwoman. "I take it Hunter won."

"Yeah." My eyes widened as Penelope did a little dance. Was she sober? Why on earth did her family let her out in public? Even Amelia was looking at her like she was an embarrassment. "Your mom's really enthusiastic, isn't she?"

He shook his head. "More like crazy."

Well... I couldn't argue the assessment. Not with her launching a cheer to spell out the name Saint George. The whole club knew she was nuts.

"Thanks for the blanket," I said.

Cat leaned closer. "Blanket?"

Oh... Um... "Lucas lent me one for my nap."

She nodded, a smile threatening to break out on her lips. "Very thoughtful of him."

He shuffled his feet and cleared his throat. "Yeah. It was Amelia's idea. And her blanket. We keep it in the car for emergency naps on long trips. But you're welcome."

Interesting... One of them wasn't telling the truth about who decided I needed to be kept warm. But why would either of them lie about it?

"So you don't have a Disney princess fetish?" I asked.

His cheeks went bright red. "No."

Cat and Maria both laughed, sharing a look that seemed to say something although I couldn't tell what. Lisa was less amused. She scowled at me like I was vermin and moved

152

around the chair to invade Lucas's personal space again.

A squeal from the side of the room told me Hunter had made it upstairs. He grinned at his aunt and draped an arm around her shoulder, then started steering her over toward us.

Great. I was still ticked at him about the night before. Even if that had been a misunderstanding, it wouldn't have happened if he hadn't been encouraging Lisa. I certainly didn't want to make nice in front of Crazy Fitz-Crazy.

My eyes snagged on Lucas as he watched the approach. I would have expected the hint of embarrassment evident in the fists he had stuffed in his pockets, but the sadness in his hunched shoulders took me by surprise.

Alerted by some extra sense that I was watching, he shifted his gaze to me for a moment before dropping it onto the ground. "Anyway..." he said. "I've got to go. Hockey. Good luck."

There was something strange in his tone, something I didn't like. But there was no examining it right then. "Thanks. Good luck to you too."

"Yeah," Hunter seconded, coming to a stop beside him. "And you should get lots of play time in with half the team busted at that party."

He smiled like he thought he was clever, but Lucas was the only one who tried to join him. My team all frowned. His aunt just looked confused. "What party?"

Hunter shook his head. "Just a bunch of high school kids being stupid. Nothing to do with Lucas. He's too smart for that kind of thing."

Of course, it didn't sound like he was complimenting his cousin. It sounded more like he was trying to say Lucas was too dull to be at something the cops would bust. Penelope didn't pick up on that though. She just smiled and said, "Oh, good."

Lucas did notice, I could tell from the flash of annoyance that crossed his face. But he didn't say anything about it. He bent to kiss his mom's cheek. "See you later, Mom."

"Alright, dear. I'll be here."

I watched Lucas go, wondering what was wrong with his mother that it didn't seem to occur to her that maybe she

153

should go with him. Sure, supporting her nephew was good. But there was something off about a woman being so enthusiastic about a nephew while simultaneously ignoring her son. She may have just considered the bonspiel more important than a random hockey match, but I couldn't remember seeing her at any of the other games either. If she was half as enthusiastic watching hockey as she was watching curling, there's no way I could have missed her.

Lisa broke off after Lucas, grabbing his arm just before he got to the stairs. She said something, then brought herself onto her toes to kiss his cheek. And the kiss was completely not like the one he'd given his mother.

He jumped away from her in surprise and stared at her for a second before his eyes flicked over to see if we were watching. We weren't. It was just me.

He looked away quickly, told her something that made her laugh, and literally ran down the stairs.

The smile Lisa sported on her way back to us turned my stomach and I had to look away from it. Cat caught my eye as I did and she raised her eyebrows. She was asking me something, but my telepathy was on the blink.

"I need to switch shoes," I said.

Giving Lisa a wide berth as I passed her, I went downstairs.

Or, I should say I went down most of the stairs. A few steps from the bottom, I found myself blocked by Lucas, who stood directly in my way while staring at the ground with an odd expression.

I stopped two stairs above him. "You lost?"

He flinched in surprise. Guess he hadn't heard my footsteps. "Um... My jacket's upstairs."

"Ah. Upstairs is that way." I pointed behind me, a pretend look of helpfulness plastered on my face.

It looked like he tried to smile, but he failed so miserably I wasn't sure. "Thanks."

I leaned my hip into the wall, folded my arms, and studied him. He looked at least as tired as he had in the morning and

154

now had a lovely gloom wrapped around him as well. "What's wrong?"

A group of people trotted down the stairs and Lucas moved to the side to let them by before he answered. It was one word, drawn out with uncertainty. "Lisa..."

"Lisa?"

He frowned and an odd crinkle scrunched his nose as he made himself look at me. "I don't know what to do about her."

Do about her? Was he really asking me for advice on his love life? Seriously? "Looks like you're doing pretty good to me."

The frown deepened. "No..."

I took a breath. "If that kiss wasn't good enough, you could try grabbing her and—"

"No!"

His cheeks lit up as I stared at him.

"Um..." he said. "I mean..."

I waited, but he didn't seem to know what he'd meant.

"You're going to be late," I told him.

"Yeah..." He went down a few steps, backwards and without taking his eyes off me. "Um... I don't suppose you could tell her..."

Something in my expression made him stop.

"I guess not."

I shook my head in agreement.

"Sorry," he said. "Never mind. I... It's just..."

"You have poor social skills?"

He ducked his head, his hair falling forward to mask his face from view. "Yeah. And... Shockingly enough, I'm not used to girls coming on to me like that. I don't really know how to be nice about letting her down. I just thought maybe you'd know what to tell her."

I stared at the top of his head. "You want to let her down?"

"Well, yeah." He looked up again, squinting in mild confusion. "Of course I do."

"Of course?" My spine straightened and I felt myself grow warm. "What do you mean, of course? If she's interested in you, you're freaking lucky!"

155

"Darcy."

"I mean, God, Lucas!"

"Darcy."

"She's cute and sweet and I know she can be a little self-absorbed but –"

"Darcy!"

The last saying of my name was more a bellowing of my name, which stopped me in my tracks so I could gape at him. He'd come up enough stairs that he was now face-to-face with me. His face was... Angry? Hurt? Why would he be hurt?

"Darcy," he said at a normal volume. "You know that's not what I meant. Don't you?"

I swallowed. "I don't know. Do I?"

His eyes moved over my face. "You should."

"Should I?"

He grunted and backed down a stair, shaking his head. "Maybe not."

While I tried to think of something to say, he turned and thumped down the stairs.

"What about your jacket?" I called after him.

He didn't turn around. "Don't need it."

I stared at the spot he'd been in for a few moments, wondering what the heck I'd missed.

Chapter Twenty-Two

I found Lucas's jacket at the end of the day, but his mom had left hours earlier because Hunter didn't have a match in the last draw. That I even noticed Hunter hadn't hung around either seriously annoyed me. Almost as much as it annoyed me to be disappointed Lucas hadn't returned after his hockey match.

Of course, the only reason I was bothered about Lucas was because now I had to drive his jacket over to his house. Otherwise, I couldn't have cared less.

I left the club with the jacket clutched in my arms. Unlike the blanket from before, I could clearly smell the owner on its worn leather. It should have stank, but it didn't. Must have been the effect of the leathery scent subduing the more appalling aspects of Lucas's old cologne.

Lisa was on the hood of my car, her knees drawn up to her chin and her arms wrapped around her furry boots. She looked little and young and lost.

"What's up?" I asked.

She hugged her legs tighter. "Mom's on a date. Jean's grounded until college. And Maria and Cat..."

She let her voice trail off. We could both guess what Maria and Cat where up to. Maria was worried about what her parents were going to do when they found out she'd skipped the SATs. She thought she could keep it from them through at least the weekend, but after that there was a good chance she'd be in lock-down too. It was understandable that she and Cat wanted some extra alone time before that happened.

"So you need a lift?"

She nodded. "Please."

I got my key out and pressed the unlock toggle. "Hop in."

She jumped down off the hood but didn't get in the car because she was looking at the jacket with an odd expression. "That looks like a guy's jacket..."

"Probably because it is." I opened my door and tossed the jacket into the back seat. "Lucas left it. Figured I'd grab it before someone ran off with it."

It wasn't like people routinely took other people's stuff from the club, but a lot of extra people were around for the bonspiel.

Lisa climbed in quickly. "Cool. His house is right by mine."

"Yeah, he said as much last night when he decided to drop me off first."

My passenger started playing with the dials on the dash as soon as the car started up. She moved the heat, changed the radio station, turned the volume up... We'd known each other too long for me to be surprised.

I turned onto Main Street, wondering which of the three bars in town Lisa's mom was in. It must have been an important date for her not to even stop by the club. When Jean and I were in preschool, she's the one who got us signed up for Little Rocks. She'd put less fervor into it after her husband left, but she was usually still around. Although now that I thought about it, she hadn't been to any of our regular season games that year either.

"Did you get to talk to Jean?" I asked. Every time I'd called either her phone or the landline, I'd gotten voicemail.

"No. Mom says she's pouting."

I grunted. It was distinctly possible.

Lisa pressed her knees into the side of the dash and tapped her palms against her legs. "Bet she'll pout even more when she finds out we did fine without her."

"Don't be ridiculous."

"Ridiculous?" She laughed. "You don't think she's been

158

eating up how upset everyone is about her wanting to leave? Well, turns out we don't need her all that much. Joke's on her."

Until that moment I hadn't spent much time thinking about anyone else's reaction to Jean going across the world for college, so her sister's bitterness caught me off guard. "I'm sure that's not why she's doing it."

"That's because you're too nice a person." She stared out the window as we turned onto the highway she lived off of. "You don't play people like that, so you assume no one else does either."

I shook my head. "No, I don't think that's it."

"But how would you know?"

She may have had a point there, but I'd known Jean for my entire life and honestly couldn't imagine that this was all a plea for attention. She just wanted things that she couldn't get here. I was coming to terms with it, but Lisa didn't sound like she was.

Poor Lisa. First her dad left town without looking back and now her sister was doing the same. It didn't quite justify running around cities with frat boys in the middle of the night, but I could certainly see motive to blow off everyone she knew to do something reckless. I'd have told her that she'd always have me, no matter what, but she'd have just rolled her eyes.

We were quiet until she piped up to say we'd reached the turn-off for Lucas's. He lived up a long, windy, path of a driveway. If the snow had been any deeper, I would have needed chains. I could see why he drove something with all-wheel drive.

The house was a large A-frame that seemed completely at home in the woods. Even the garage looked woodsy, being made from the same lumber as the house. Belatedly, it occurred to me that this could be the garage Hunter lived over. It looked like there was enough room up there for a small apartment.

Despite being in the middle of nowhere, both the main house and the garage were decorated with an array of Christmas lights that lit the area in front of them brighter than the street lamps kept my street.

159

"Whoa," Lisa said. "Someone wants to make sure Santa knows where to stop."

The lights weren't garish or anything, just bright. They reminded me of that movie where the guy wanted his house to be visible from space. Lucas's mom must have been as enthusiastic about Christmas as she was about curling.

While I stared at the lights, Lisa grabbed the jacket out of the back seat. "I'll take it up. You stay here."

She managed to say all that like it was a favor, not her bossing me around or marking territory. Much as I disliked the thought of Lucas as Lisa's territory, I let it go. It was cold out and I'd be happier sitting in the heat. Besides, it wasn't like I wanted to talk to Lucas anyway.

But much as I didn't want to talk to him, I still found myself staring at the front door of his house as Lisa knocked on it. She shuffled her feet, probably trying to keep them warm, as she waited. And waited...

After the second pounding, the door opened.

It wasn't Lucas's body propping it open though. It wasn't Lucas listening to what Lisa said and then looking over at me. It wasn't Lucas who ushered her inside before stepping out on the porch.

It was Hunter.

He walked out to the car, seeming oblivious to the fact that his tissue-thin sweater was too light for temperatures well under freezing. The wind whipped around his hair, lifting it up and giving it a disheveled look that would sell for serious money in a salon.

He got into the passenger side without asking, folded his arms, and stared at the dash. The way the lights hit his tense jaw and furrowed eyebrows gave him a sinister air and kept me from saying anything as I waited for him to speak.

"I didn't take Lisa to the city. I didn't invite her. I didn't even see her because you have to be eighteen to get into the club my cousin was playing."

He said all of it to the dust coating the dashboard. Something about that made me believe him more than if he'd

160

been meeting my eyes.

I swallowed, feeling miserable for attacking him when he hadn't even known Lisa was in town. I nodded silently.

"If you'd told me what was going on, I'd have helped." He reached over and found my hand. "You didn't have to drag Lucas into it."

My pulse picked up as he stroked my fingers with his thumb. "I didn't drag him. He was there when I found out."

"You're lucky he didn't bail half-way there."

I tugged my hand away, using the dial on the heater as an excuse. "I'd have just hit him over the head and kept driving with him in the trunk."

Hunter laughed. "That's the spirit."

Was it? "Why do you care so much about making me think less of him?"

"Isn't that obvious?"

I folded my arms and tried to look fierce. "No."

He laughed again and, so fast I didn't have a single warning, yanked me toward him and started kissing me.

It was nice. Warm. A lot better than the last time we'd kissed. But it wasn't good enough to make me forget I'd asked him a question.

He didn't want to let me pull back, but I put force into it and managed to escape.

To make my point clearer, I got out of the car completely.

"That didn't answer my question," I said as cold wrapped around me and brushed over my lips in sharp contrast to Hunter's kiss. "And you haven't told me why Lisa would have thought you were inviting her into the city if you weren't. Exactly what did you tell her?"

Leaning over the gearshift, he grinned up at me. "Which question do you want me to answer?"

Ugh. I jammed my hands into my hair.

There was a movement on the porch. Lucas. He was even less dressed for the weather than Hunter. Flannel pants, short sleeved tee, and no shoes. He looked like he'd already gone to bed before we showed up making noise. Or before Lisa showed

161

up in his room...

I slammed the car door and went up to the house. Faint sounds of carols drifted through the cracked door. "Where's Lisa?"

Lucas looked pained. "She's with my mother."

Behind me, my car's engine shut off. I assumed because of Hunter. "Wow, you let her talk to your mom? You really aren't interested in her, are you?"

He shrugged and gave me a tiny smile. "I'd answer, but I don't want to be yelled at."

As Hunter climbed out of the car, I went into the house. The door opened into a foyer decorated with family photos. I recognized a younger Lucas easily and almost laughed at the way his ears stuck out. "Growing your hair out was a good move."

"Thanks."

He shut the door, even though he had to be aware his cousin was outside, and edged toward the archway out of the entryway, seeming to want me away from the photos. That, naturally, made me more interested in them. There were quite a few of young big-eared Lucas, a lot of Amelia, and several of a girl who was obviously related to both of them. Michelle... And there was a man I didn't know but assumed was Lucas's dad. Some pictures of Hunter. And... "Is that your mom?"

"Um... Yeah."

Penelope was standing with a curling team, all sporting USA jackets. She'd gone to the World Championships?

I parted my lips in preparation to ask Lucas about that, but he'd given up on waiting for me to be done and was already half-way across a large family room dominated by a huge tree. I started after him, but then stopped and gaped at the tree. It was at least twelve feet tall. Maybe more. "I don't think I've ever seen a tree that big that wasn't outdoors or in a mall."

"Yeah... Mom gets a little obsessive." He flopped down on the sofa, landing in the corner in a graceless sprawl.

The smell of baking cookies coming from a room over was tempting, but when I heard the door opening I sat down on the

162

couch as fast as I could. Lucas's lips twisted in an ironic smile at the action. It was almost enough to get me to stand up again. Almost. I folded my legs into a lotus position, taking up as much space as possible, and grabbed a throw-pillow to hug. It was soft and covered with dancing reindeer.

Hunter put too much energy into closing the door and stomped into the room, giving Lucas an evil glower. Lucas didn't seem to care.

It went on for a few moments, the guys staring at each other, until I had to drop my eyes and watch the reindeer instead. Then Hunter said, "Didn't I send a girl to your room?"

The couch moved as Lucas shifted. "Yes, I believe you did. Thanks."

He did not, of course, sound grateful.

"What?" Hunter asked. "Did you not know what to do with her?"

My eyes were wide, but I kept them on the pillow. Being part of this conversation didn't seem like a great idea, but running away screaming would attract a lot of attention.

"Well, gee," Lucas said dryly, "is it like what you do when you have them trapped in cars? I don't have quite as much experience with that as you."

Suddenly the blood was rushing through my ears loud enough to drown out the music from the kitchen. Maybe if I ran away without screaming they wouldn't notice? The vague hint of Hunter's taste still on my tongue made my stomach roll and I wondered where the nearest bathroom was.

"Never will at this rate," Hunter said.

Lucas snorted. "Whatever."

"Brilliant comeback."

I sneaked a peak at Lucas. He was about to say something, but noticed me and stilled. When he did speak, I don't think he said what he had meant to say before. "Lisa is awesome, Hunter, but she's fifteen. Not to mention..."

He trailed off and looked at me.

I raised my eyebrows. "Not to mention what?"

"That she has an early draw again tomorrow."

163

"Shit." I tossed the pillow aside and got to my feet. "I thought we didn't play until second."

Hunter sighed. "No, you got boned. We were talking about it earlier."

In that case, I needed to be in bed half an hour ago. "I would have kept the stupid jacket in my car if I'd known that. Lisa!"

I had to walk to the kitchen before I got her attention. She sat at the counter eating sugar cookies and watching Lucas's mom decorate an army of gingerbread men. Penelope smiled at me when I came in, looking so sweet and kind that I wondered if she was actually a twin. Lisa scowled.

"We have early draw," I said. "I've gotta go to bed."

"Oh." She frowned toward Lucas, who had followed me without me realizing it. Dang, but he was quiet on bare feet.

She was obviously hoping Lucas would offer to drive her down to her house later, but he'd had a long day too and didn't say a word.

With a sad sigh, Lisa grabbed an extra cookie and told Penelope good night.

"Night girls," she said, beaming at us like she hadn't noticed any of the tension that walked into the room with me and Lucas.

"Darcy," Lucas said as I headed out the front door. He touched my arm, lightly, just enough to get me to stop. "If I don't make it there in time tomorrow, good luck."

I smiled. "Thanks. Don't worry about it. You need sleep."

He shrugged. "So do you."

"Good point." As if bidden, a yawn crept forth.

Lisa made an annoyed sound from near the car. "I thought we were in a hurry."

I smiled at Lucas again. He hadn't even glanced toward Lisa, which probably aggravated her more than me taking my time did. "How did hockey go?"

"Alright." He shrugged. "I scored."

"Really?"

He smiled and shifted his weight between his feet. "We still

164

lost."

"Naturally. It's what you do."

We looked at each other for a few moments as Lisa crunched through the snow. Then I shook myself, gave him an extra smile, and got my ass home before I did anything stupid.

TO: jeansmith@merytonhs.com
FROM: darcybennet@merytonhs.com
SUBJECT: Miss You

Hey. I tried to call several times today but no one ever answered. I hope that just means you're super-grounded, not that there's something seriously wrong.

I know things have been awful lately. I'm sorry for that. I love you. And miss you like crazy. And, no, that's not just because I don't really enjoying skipping. Although I don't. You don't get to do nearly enough while standing there in the house as everyone else curls. There's too much time to think.

We did okay today. Lost one but won the other three. But we play Ellen first thing in the morning and if we win, we'll have to play them again in the finals. If we don't, I'm not sure we'll make it to finals.

I'm all sorts of confused about a bunch of stuff. I wish I could talk to you about it! But I'm betting I'll be just as confused on Monday. So, assuming you're not grounded from school, I'll talk to you then... Right now I need to get some sleep because tomorrow's going to start way too early.

Love, Darcy

TO: darcybennet@myrtonhs.com
FROM: cnetherfield@sotc.com
SUBJECT: RE: Lucas Fitzwilliam

Oh my gosh, Darce! Charlie finally got back to me on the Lucas thing.

You know his sister died, right? Well, it happened while he was at Nationals. Like she was going to see him play and went off the road and everyone was wondering where she was for hours before the Highway Patrol managed to get hold of someone who knew the whole family was watching curling. (He sent a copy of an article about it I'll attach to this.)

Charlie says there was debate if Lucas should have left or not since he couldn't do anything about his sister being dead, but his niece would have been, what, three? Four maybe? She was in the car too and she was really hurt. She was in ICU and everything. Lucas is her world, she would have needed him. And, well, I have to admit that if it was Charlie, I'd leave too. And I probably wouldn't want to curl anymore any time soon either.

So... Does that completely mess with your idea of who Lucas Fitzwilliam is or is it what you were expecting?

See you in the morning, Cat

LOCAL GIRL DIES IN HIGHWAY MISHAP

Michelle Marie Fitzwilliam was a frequent sight around town, from the ice cream counter at Beckman's where she worked to the frozen floors of the skate rink and the curling house. You might say that her life revolved around ice, but oddly enough, her mid-February roadway death had nothing to do with the slippery substance.

The morning of Michelle's passing was clear and bright, the temperatures unseasonably warm. She was traveling to Bemidji to watch her younger brother compete in the Junior National Curling Championships, a tournament that Michelle had won several years previously, prior to an unexpected pregnancy at age seventeen.

Michelle was killed instantly when her car crashed through a rail on Highway 2. Her young daughter, who was with her, is currently being treated for severe injuries but is expected to survive.

Michelle's service will be at Saint Marks this coming Saturday. In lieu of flowers, her family has requested donations be made to the National Curling Association.

Chapter Twenty-Three

There was a foot of snow on the ground when I woke up. I stared at it and considered going back to bed. I hadn't fallen asleep until about three hours before the alarm went off and shoveling my way out of the driveway seemed like a daunting task, to say the least. Snuggling back under the covers with Penny the Purple Penguin seriously tempted me.

But curling doesn't stop just because there's snow on the ground, so I subjected myself to a shower and grabbed the shovel from the garage.

I stopped in the driveway, feeling stupid. I could shovel off our property, but the roads hadn't been touched yet. Probably wouldn't be until after the sun came up, which would be after I was supposed to be at the club.

Crap.

My poor little car couldn't handle all this. Mom had made sure I knew how to get chains on my tires, but I'd never had to use them before and wasn't terribly confident in my ability to do so now. I wasn't even sure this was a situation they'd really help in.

The shovel clanked onto the cement floor as I threw it down in disgust. Yanking off my mittens, I dug into my pocket for my phone. First step, call the club and make sure we weren't on a delay anyway. Step two...

Headlights swung around the corner and my fingers paused on the menu as they hobbled toward me. Was that..?

Yes, yes it was. Lucas's beat up old Outback was limping down the road.

It rolled to a grinding stop in the middle of the road and Lisa leaned out of the passenger window. "Come on! We'll be late!"

Without thinking twice, I grabbed my mittens, yanked the garage door down, and ran over.

Something about Lucas needing to charge in to save people was forming on my tongue when I opened the door, but it faded out when I realized there were already two people in the backseat.

"Jean!" I grinned as I climbed in next to Hunter. He'd managed to snag the middle seat, but I leaned around him to beam at Jean. "Your mom let you out?"

Lisa laughed. "She can't stop her until the roads get ploughed. The truck's in the shop!"

Jean thumped the back of her chair. "I got permission. I'm not allowed to play, but I'm allowed to cheer."

"Awesome!" I looked forward even though Hunter tried to catch my eye and put my hands on Lucas's headrest. "Thanks for the ride, Lucas. I had no idea what I was going to do."

Hunter put a hand on my knee. I went still, not sure what to do about it. There wasn't anywhere to move to get away from him and if I said something then I'd be drawing everyone's attention to it. I jerked my leg over as far as I could, hoping he'd take the hint. He didn't.

"Normally it wouldn't be a problem," I said, babbling. "Because our SUV's really good on snow. But Mom and Shel and the twins are visiting Shel's parents... It's his mom's birthday..."

Hunter frowned. "They think that's more important than your bonspiel?"

I shrugged. "She's really old. She might not have many more."

"Yeah, right." He rolled his eyes. "My grandmother's been pulling that line since before I was born."

We slid to a stop at a blinking red intersection. Had the

power gone out in this part of town? If it was off at the club, there wasn't any point in us going there. "Did anyone call and make sure the spiel's still on?"

"Yeah," Lucas answered. "You really think I'd bother with all this if it was closed?"

I smiled a little. "Guess not. Sorry, it's early. I temporarily forgot your aversion to going out of your way for people."

He twisted around to smile at me. He stopped smiling when he noticed Hunter's hand.

The car lurched forward as soon as Lucas was facing forward again.

The rest of the ride, the only people who said anything were Lisa and Hunter. I'm not sure what was in Jean's head. Maybe she was sleepy. But me... I kept my eyes trained out the window to keep myself from staring at Lucas.

Something had changed between him and me. I wasn't sure exactly what or when, but... When I'd written to Jean that I was confused, I'd mostly meant that I was confused about Lucas. I'd been paying way too much attention to him the last few... Days? Weeks?

Shit. Yes, the last few weeks. I hadn't even noticed I was doing it, but I'd been looking at him too often in class. I'd been talking to him more than I should have. I'd felt disappointed whenever he wasn't in a place he was supposed to be. I'd even been reading his stupid articles in the paper.

But Hunter was the one I'd been flirting with. Hunter was the one who'd kissed me. Hunter was the one with his hand on my knee even though I'd scooted as close to the door as I could get...

We pulled into the parking lot of the club. There were a surprisingly large number of cars, a couple of them wearing chains. I got out of the car as soon as we were stopped and rushed into the building. It was sheer chaos. People were running around trying to figure out who was here and who wasn't and what we should do about it. Was it fair to penalize anyone not on time for their draw? Or should they redo the schedule somehow? How late could we stay here tonight? If the playoff matches were moved to tomorrow, would the out-of-towners be okay with that? Were any of the out-of-towners here to ask? Half the organizers were panicked. The other half hadn't made it in yet.

And, worst of all, there was no coffee. That could start a riot.

I went into the kitchen and found an unopened canister in the back of one of the cabinets. It was the emergency stash. Most of the club didn't know where it was, but last season I'd been on a rec team with the woman in charge of stocking the kitchen.

Starting a pot of caffeine only bought me so much time though. Hunter came in as I set it up. He leaned against the counter across the kitchen from me, waiting for me to finish.

"You still mad at me?" he asked. "Cause I can drag that little brat in here and have her back me up. I did not take, invite, or otherwise encourage her to take her little trip the other night."

"I believe you." I hopped up on the counter beside the coffee pot. "Lisa gets enthusiastic. It sort of warps her perceptions of what people are saying."

"Then what's the attitude about?" He straightened and crossed the space separating us. He put his hands on either side of me and I suddenly saw the error of jumping up where I could be trapped. "What's wrong? Is it Ellen?"

"Why would your girlfriend be the problem?"

He shook his head. "Not my girlfriend. I told you that. We messed around a little, but that's as far as it went."

"Messed around?" I leaned back, away from the scent of mint on his breath. "And what do you want to do with me? The same?"

He frowned.

"I'm not a casual hook-up kind of girl, Hunter."

His gaze dropped to the side but he stayed where he was, still pinning me down. He stayed like that for a few moments, long enough for me to start feeling seriously edgy. Just as I was about to shove him away so I could move, he looked up. "So, what, you want to go steady?"

I stared at him. "You spent that whole time trying to remember that phrase, didn't you?"

He glowered. "No."

Yeah, he did. I shook my head. "No, I don't want to 'go steady' with you."

"Then what do you want?"

He leaned closer, invading my space until I didn't have any left. Our lips touched and I tensed up. I couldn't back away any further, but I didn't have to kiss him back.

It didn't take him long to figure out that this approach wasn't working. He pulled back and frowned at me. "Why won't you tell me what's wrong?"

I put my hands on his shoulders and pushed him a little. Luckily, he went without a fight because I never could have forced him if he wasn't willing. When there was enough space, I got my butt off the counter and put some distance between us. "Nothing's wrong. I just..."

"Just..." He folded his arms and waited with an impatient scowl.

I took a deep breath and went for it. "I just don't want to kiss you."

"Why not?"

Why not? I stared at him, not having a clue how to answer a question like that. "So, what, you assume everyone on Earth wants to make-out with you?"

He shrugged. "Not guys. Or lesbians. You're not a lesbian, are you?"

"No, I'm not a lesbian." It was a cruel time for it but I couldn't keep myself from laughing at his confusion. "You're unbelievable."

"I'm unbelievable?" he stammered. "You've been leading me on for weeks and suddenly you're just not interested?"

I stopped laughing. "I'm sorry. I wasn't trying to be a tease. I swear."

"Whatever."

He brushed by me on his way out the door, knocking my

shoulder hard enough to send me into the counter.

"Yeah, whatever," I said to myself. "Asshole."

My hip stung as I crossed back to the coffee pot. The water trickled too slowly, taking too much time to kill the karaf. I drummed my fingers on the countertop as I waited. Even though I hadn't had any caffeine yet, my body buzzed with energy all of a sudden. It was all I could do not to run out of the kitchen. I had no idea what I wanted to do once I left, but the desire to run was almost too great to ignore.

Maybe I wanted to kill Hunter. Or possibly kiss him... Or maybe, just maybe, I wanted to kiss someone else...

Carol strutted into the room in new, and very tight, curling gear. Unlike everyone else in the building, she didn't look like she'd woken up too early. She was like one of those movie characters who sprung out of bed chipper and already wearing cosmetics.

"Mmm, coffee," she purred.

"Yep." Could I hand coffee duty over to her? No. She'd pour some for herself, then leave the pot and not even tell anyone it was there.

"So you were in here with Hunter for a while."

I took a breath and folded my arms to keep my fingers still. "Not too long."

"Long enough." She gave me a very suggestive wink. "Good work with him. Ellen will be pissed, but you guys have way more chemistry than they did."

"Oh, we're not—"

"It's Jean I can't believe. Moving on already? Talk about turn-around times."

I stopped mid-sentence to process what Carol had said over me. "Moving on? What?"

"She didn't tell you yet?" Carol shrugged. "Guess she's been busy, what breaking up with Adam, visiting prison, hooking up with Adam's best friend..."

Hook... "What?"

She laughed. "You really do need that coffee, don't you? I think it's done."

"Uh huh." I was way too hot, yet covered in chill bumps as I turned and looked at the coffee pot without really seeing it. The smell of it was turning my stomach, so drinking it was about the last thing I wanted to do.

The first thing I wanted to do was to have left the kitchen before Carol showed up. What she'd just said... It couldn't be true. She was just trying to shake me. Right?

"I mean, I've known Lucas was crazy about Jean for a while," she said. "That's why I gave up on him. But my poor brother had no clue until he saw them dancing together last night."

Okay... They had both been at the dance. Maybe even danced with each other. But that's not weird. Friends do that. It didn't mean Jean had bailed on the guy she'd been crushing on all year. "I don't know what you saw, but Jean's really into Adam."

Carol laughed again. "Yeah? Well, you obviously don't know what I saw or you wouldn't say that. And, FYI, it wasn't just me. Adam saw it too. It's all over that they were arguing about it at that party they went to when the cops showed up."

I shook my head, refusing to believe it.

But Lucas did carry pictures of Jean around on his phone. And he'd spent four hours in the car fetching a girl he wasn't interested in, but who was Jean's sister. And, yeah, he'd made his friend ask her to the dance, but he'd said all along that Jean and Adam wouldn't last together. Had said all along that Jean deserved someone better. Could he have meant himself?

Coffee sloshed in the pot as I carried it out to the stand they'd set up for it yesterday and thunked it down next to a stack of disposable cups.

Where was Lucas? I had to find him, had to reassure myself that Carol was full of it. But when my eyes finally landed on him, my insides crumbled.

He and Jean leaned close to each other, whispering and laughing about something. They were in their own little world, the rest of the room not even registering for them. And that's when I knew Carol was right and the guy I'd just realized I

175

liked was totally into my best friend.

Chapter Twenty-Four

Fog coated my brain as I stepped onto the ice for my match against Ellen. I clung to it, wrapping it around me to protect me from my emotions.

I didn't have any right to be upset. It's not like I'd ever done anything to make Lucas think I could stand being around him, let alone might want more than friendship from him. And as far as Jean knew, I could hardly stand the guy. All I ever did was complain about him.

I'd been a complete bitch. I had absolutely no business feeling miserable because I wasn't the one he whispered to, that I wasn't the one whose cheek was warmed by his breath, whose hair was brushed aside by his movements, whose –

I cut myself off. Maybe later, when I was alone, I'd let myself think about all that. Let myself cry my way to sleep over it. But for now I had some curling to do.

I shoved all my feelings down and smiled at my teammates. "Alright, let's do this."

They smiled back, nervous. Jean would say something encouraging, but I didn't know what it would be. I wasn't Jean. Never would be. Shouldn't be trying to be.

Ellen slid to stop beside me. "I'd be happy to take your concession now."

"Nah." I shrugged. "We got up, might as well play."

"Have it your way." She held out her hand. "Good curling."

"Good curling," I said, hoping I didn't sound as snide as she had.

I shook with her lead and second, but when I came to Carol her expression made me pause. "Good curling?"

Her eyes flicked to my hand, which was still down at my side rather than being offered to her and she raised her eyebrows. "If your real skip is out because of an STD she gave my brother before she dumped him, I'm going to kill her."

I put my hand out without a word. No way was I dignifying that with a denial.

She spent a few seconds staring at it, then shook.

Lisa frowned as she edged closer to me. "What was that about?"

Shrugging, I pretended not to know.

The vice-skips flipped the coin and we took hammer. As I slid down to the end of the sheet, I promised myself I wouldn't look up at the spectators. But, of course, the second I turned around I did.

At the very front of the glass, Jean waved, smiling in encouragement. Beside her, Lucas stood with folded arms. He nodded and mouthed, "Good luck."

For a few heartbeats, I let myself look back at him.

Then Ellen came up beside me. If we'd been on skates, she almost definitely would have done a hockey stop that would have left me covered in shaved ice. But curling shoes don't do that, so she had to resort to glaring at me.

Neither of us said anything, but she made a big deal about sending a flirtatious wave to the next sheet over, where Hunter was. When he waved back, she gave me a smirk that made me want to smack her even though I didn't give a fig if she wanted to get it on with Hunter or not.

As she stopped trying to rile me long enough to set up a shot for her lead, Hunter raised his eyebrows at me in question. I ignored him.

Despite a pair of horrible throws from Lisa, we took two points in the first end. I nodded at Maria as she went down to the scoreboard to mark them, but avoided looking at anyone else.

"I'm sorry," Lisa said as we passed. She'd apologized earlier too and I gave her the same little smile I did before.

"It's just the first end. You'll do better next one."

Except that was a lie. If anything, she did worse. Once you get it into your head that you suck, you start to even if you didn't really before.

"It's okay," I called down to her. Carol smiled an oily smile and said something that didn't carry down to me, but which made Maria grip the handle of her broom like she wanted to hit the little curly haired bitch over the head with it.

It really was alright. Her stone hadn't gone anywhere near where'd I'd called, but it had landed in a useful position. That wasn't good enough for her though, not today. Her next shot missed all of Ellen's rocks and smacked into the boards behind me. Way too hard. The voices in her head were killing her.

Maria made up for it with a brilliant takeout and while we did lose the end, we only gave them one.

Near the end of the fifth, the lights flickered and Ted Peterson, the club president, came out. "Everyone? Hello? We have an announcement."

He waited for everyone to settle down, which took a little while because we were all looking at each other and going, "What's going on?" We weren't used to people interrupting us mid-game.

"You may have noticed we've had a bit of snow."

There was a scattering of confused laughter.

"Yeah..." He winced. "There's going to be a few more feet of it. The bands have shifted and they're saying we have about an hour before it hits here, hard. Which means we're going to have to stop curling and get home."

More traded looks. Exasperated grunts. Insistences that we'd be fine and please to just let us stay here.

But none of that made a difference. "You kids can finish this end and one more, then we're out of here. We'll figure out what to do about the rest of the games later."

There were protests, of course, but Ted shook his head at them. "Anyone who wants to argue about it is free to forfeit the last two ends and talk to me in the warm room."

And then he left.

Everyone stared at the door for a few seconds, then turned back to their games. What else were we supposed to do?

Ellen muttered to herself as she sat up Carol's second shot. My team had the hammer this end and we were still up by one. On top of that, we had shot rock right then and it was pretty well guarded. Things hadn't been looking great for her before the announcement about the shortened game and they certainly weren't looking any better now.

Carol slid out of the hack light and as the stone crossed the hogline, I let myself think it was going to end short. But her sweepers did their job and the late-end ice had picked up speed. The rock slid around the guards and curled right into my shot rock, knocking it back so that Carol's rock became the new point-scorer.

"Same shot," I yelled down to Maria, putting my broom in the exact same spot Ellen had used.

"Yeah, good luck with that," Ellen muttered. "You know she always screws up her release. It'll never curl right."

"Hold on!" I called. Ellen was right. Maria's shots never curled exactly like they should. But that was fine. I didn't need it to. I moved, putting my broom down in an entirely different spot. "Double take-out!"

Even from the house, I knew Maria had just gone pale. But she didn't argue. She gave me a confident nod and lined up.

She pulled back... Slid forward, fast and heavy. She released and the rock flew down the ice. Perfect... Perfect... "Line's beautiful!"

"Weight's great!" Lisa called, zipping down the ice ahead of the stone.

Slam! The rock hit hard enough that the guys on the sheets to either side of us looked over to see what had happened. Then it smacked into the shot rock and sent that one out of the rings too. Text book! "Good shot, Maria!"

"Well, hell," Ellen said. She shook her head. "Should have kept my mouth shut."

"Yeah, you should have." I grinned at her. She was frustrated as anything, but there was a new respect in the way she glared at me.

It took a few minutes for Ellen to decide what she wanted to do. She needed a steal this end, but she didn't have a single rock in the house and I had three of them. Her own rocks were set up as guards. If she tried to bump them into the house, they'd just hit my stones and move them closer to the center. If she went around them... Well, it would be tough to get around both them and my rocks. So, again, she'd probably just move me into better position unless she was really, really lucky.

They decided to try to go through a narrow gap between the guards, slide between two of the rocks I had in the house, and try to freeze against the shot rock.

Personally, I wasn't sure what I would have done in their place. The shot Ellen called was hard. Really hard. But I didn't see anything easier that had any hope of scoring them points. Most likely, I would have given up on the idea of a steal and tried to minimize the damage.

I glanced upstairs as Ellen slid down to the hack. All eyes were on us. None of the other games were this close. In fact, Hunter's team was busy accepting a concession from their opponents.

Lucas shook his head. He didn't like Ellen's call either, but I wasn't sure if that was because he thought it was too risky or because he didn't want her to score.

As soon as Ellen's foot left the hack, I knew she'd missed her shot. I think she knew it too because she already wore a snarl of annoyance when the rock left her hand and she didn't bother directing the sweepers. Her stone's line was closer than I'd thought at first, but the stone still nicked the side of one of her guards. It took that rock's place and the guard moved forward. It made it into the house but, like I'd predicted, all it did was nudge one of my stones closer to the center.

Maria glanced at me. "Guard it?"

"Guard it!"

I went down to take my shot and threw a high guard to plug

the hole, giving Ellen even less of a chance on her next shot.

Ellen took even more time on the next call. If she missed again, then this shot could be her last of the game. She'd be down five going into the last end and I was pretty sure she'd concede rather than make us play it out. Especially since there was a decent chance I'd take an extra point if she didn't stop the game before my final shot of the end.

Between the normal suspense of an important game and the knowledge that everyone in the club was watching us, even the teams who were still playing, my insides were a quivering mass of anxiety. But there was nothing I could do other than wait and see how much brilliance my opponent could pull out.

Eventually, after a lot of deliberation, she tried the same shot as before.

I didn't breathe as she left the hack and released the rock, perfectly this time... I didn't move a muscle as the stone curled down the ice looking just right... I could hardly stand to look as it got closer to the gap in the guards.

I don't think anyone some much as breathed as it slid past the newest guard.

The click as it skimmed the second guard carried through the whole rink.

It was barely a hit, but it was enough.

We were laying four.

Ellen banged her fist against the ice.

She bent her head and her shoulders shook. But when she stood up a second later, her face was devoid of expression.

She held her hand out to me. "Good game."

Most of Team Nemisis got off the ice quick, but their second stayed behind. Hiro was all of five feet nothing and had dainty Asian features that made her look like a fragile little doll, but when she wasn't curling, she was fencing. She was probably the most dangerous member of her team, so it was lucky she was also the nicest. "I'm sorry everyone's all tense. We've had kind of a weird week."

Lisa rolled her eyes. "Who hasn't?"

Word to that.

But we all smiled to show no hard feelings, at least not toward Hiro, and got the ice cleaned as quickly as we could. I tried not to wonder if Lucas was still watching and succeeded in not looking up to check.

I followed my teammates into the warm room and was instantly attacked by the half-monsters. They were screaming, "Darcy won! Darcy won!"

I laughed at their chant, but shushed them. "Now you know taunting's not nice."

"What's taunting?" Elijah asked, though I was pretty sure he knew.

Mom moved through the mill to put a hand on each of the boys. "Calm down, both of you. I said you could go congratulate your sister, not rip her to shreds."

I hugged the twins until they squirmed, which is usually the easiest way to get them to leave me alone. True to tendency, they barreled off the second I let go and I was able to give Mom a quick squeeze. "What are you doing here?"

"I can't watch my baby girl curl?"

I left an arm around her shoulders and used to it guide her toward the lockers. "Sure. When your mother-in-law isn't turning even more ancient."

"That was yesterday. We got up early to make it here, but then got slowed with the snow."

I nodded. They were lucky none of the roads they needed had been closed.

"Change quick and we can get out of here."

I nodded again and ran into the locker room.

When I came back out in my snow boots, Shel had joined Mom and they had the boys trapped between them. And they were talking to Lucas.

I started toward them, but Hunter appeared in my way halfway there. He gave me a wide smile. It was tempting to push past him but I decided to be polite. "Hey, Hunter. Congratulations."

"Congratulations yourself," he said. "That win was epic."

I shrugged. The win had more to do with Ellen's mistakes

183

than with my skills. "Thanks."

"Listen..." He reached out to brush my hair and I inched back. "I know things can get weird during bonspiels. Lots of stress and stuff. But... I really like you, Darcy."

Ugh. Why was it Hunter saying this? Couldn't he tell that I was biting back screaming at him for being the wrong cousin? But the right cousin... He was still talking to Shel, but Jean had come up beside him. She said something and he laughed. And my heart whimpered.

"I like you too, Hunter," I said, forcing my attention to him. "I just don't like-like you."

He winced at the elementary-school phrasing. "Bet I could change your mind."

I shook my head.

"Please?"

His eyes were wide with pleading and although I still wasn't interested in him that way, I started to feel bad about it. It wasn't his fault I was obsessing over someone else. And since that someone else wasn't reciprocating... Hunter was gorgeous. Definitely more attractive than Lucas in the general sense. Though not as smart or witty or.... I shook my head again. No, it wouldn't be fair to string Hunter along. Not now that I knew I'd be doing it.

His shoulders slumped. "How about we talk later? Let me think of something, put together the perfect date."

It wouldn't be a perfect date, not if he was the one I was with on it. But saying that seemed cruel. "I'll see you around."

He let me go, even though I hadn't agreed to anything.

I said goodbye to Lucas and Jean and my teammates, then I let Shel drive me home.

TO: darcypryce@merytonhs.com
FROM: jeanbennett@merytonhs.com
SUBJECT: RE: Miss You

I've missed you too! ::hugs::

We didn't really get time to talk. What are you confused about?

Love, Jean

TO: jeanbennett@merytonhs.com
FROM: darcypryce@merytonhs.com
SUBJECT: RE: Miss You

Never mind. I figured it out.

See you after the blizzard!

Love, Darcy

Chapter Twenty-Five

Fears and predictions to the contrary, the snow didn't hit us until close to nightfall. But it hit strong and fast. By morning, we had three new feet piled onto what we'd had already.

My alarm never went off because we knew before bed that school would be canceled. I slept until after noon. I told everyone it was because I was short on sleep from the last two mornings, but in reality it was because I was up most of the night replaying every conversation I'd ever had with Lucas and analyzing every little detail. Had he really been acting like a jerk when we first met or had I misunderstood him?

For example, there was this time he said something about how he preferred hockey to curling because it was more of a challenge. At the time, I classed that as an attack on my sport. But that was before I'd even known he played, let alone knew how well he played. Maybe he was just saying that hockey doesn't come as naturally to him so it gave him more room for drastic improvement. That wasn't really the same as dismissing curling as too easy, was it? Anyone who'd been to Nationals knows curling isn't easy.

Or maybe I was making excuses now because at some point I'd realized his eyes looked like polished mahogany. Because I'd noticed the way my heartbeat sped up whenever I got close to him. Because I'd picked up on the fact that days when I didn't see him just didn't shine like the days when I had. Because it had finally sunk into my brain that I was crazy about him.

Not that it mattered. Whatever he meant, I'd said the things I'd said. I'd snubbed him. I'd attacked him. I'd told him he was a horrible person because he'd left a bonspiel over his sister's death and his niece's hospitalization. I'd generally treated him like a fungus. He'd have to be stupid to want me after all that. Stupid enough that I'd have probably changed my mind about wanting him.

Of course, he didn't want me. He wanted Jean. Which just proved that he was smart enough to be lust-worthy.

It was almost enough to make me go back to bed, but the twins were playing in the snow outside my window and making enough noise to wake a coma patient.

I put on my snow things and joined the half-monsters out in the frozen wonderland that used to be our yard. They were cute, all bundled up and making tunnels in snow deeper than they were tall. We spent hours digging. Mom brought us hot chocolate, but we didn't go inside once. Not until she came out and said we had to. Party pooper. Couldn't she see her kids were bonding?

She wouldn't even let us play inside. She said the twins needed baths. Like snow was dirty or something.

I changed clothes in a pout and went to find my other sibling. If any of my bothers needed bathing, it was Kevin, but he was plopped on the sofa in the den playing a video game. Looked like he was killing zombies.

He didn't glance as me as I sat, but he paused the game to stare when I asked, "Can I play?"

"Um... Sure." His chin jerked toward the console. "Grab a controller."

He saved his game and went into the two player menu.

"Can I be a zombie?" I asked.

He laughed. "Nope. Humans only."

"Bummer." Controller in hand, I sat down again.

"Yeah." He grunted. "There is a game where you can be a zombie, but it's kinda sucky. I keep hoping someone will make a better one."

"Learn to program."

He snorted. "Yeah, sure."

The game started up and I started pressing buttons. It took all of ten seconds for me to die.

With a head-shake, Kev paused the game. He explained the controls before he restarted it and that time I made it an entire minute before meeting my demise.

"Guess video games still aren't my thing," I said.

"Nah, you just need practice."

Showing more patience than I'd thought he was capable of, he rebooted again. And again. And again. Until eventually I was lasting long enough to feel like I was playing the game rather than instantly committing suicide.

We were quiet as we played, but somehow I felt closer to him than I had since we were little. It was all very guy-like.

Mom busted that up too. I was starting to think she was getting jealous, a suspicion that was fed fuel when she insisted on playing spades as soon as the twins were in bed.

We won, me and Mom. But it was possible the guys let us, Kevin because he didn't care enough not to and Shel because he wanted to see Mom happy. I couldn't blame him, she's awfully cute when she's won something. And he did kind of owe her for the birthday trip. Shel's mother can't stand Mom and has never tried to hide it.

It was a good day, but my thoughts started up again as soon as I laid down. Lucas lived right next to Jean. Had he gone down the hill to see her? She wouldn't have turned him away, she would have let him in. Did they keep their distance out of respect to Lisa and Adam? Or not?

After an hour of painful imagining, I got up and took a sleeping pill. It knocked me out until Mom pounded on the door telling me to come have lunch.

TO: darcybennet@merytonhs.com
FROM: lucasfitzwilliam@merytonhs.com
SUBJECT: English

Did you see that? We have an assignment! Doesn't Mrs L know we're supposed to be building snowmen? Doesn't she know what the words 'snow day' mean?

Anyway... I don't have my English book with me. (What? I didn't lug it home just because I didn't have any reason to Friday? Clearly, I'm trying to fail.) Do you have yours?

-Lucas

TO: lucasfitzwilliam@merytonhs.com
FROM: darcybennet@merytonhs.com
SUBJECT: RE: English

By some miracle, yes, I have my book! I'll scan the pages for you. It's just a few lame poems we're supposed to record our reactions to. (Or the reactions she wants us to have. I don't think she wants my honest "All this sentiment's making me gag!" one.) It shouldn't take long, you'll be back to your snowmen in no time. Besides, you're not limited by the sun like the rest of us. Not with all those lights on your house!

-D

Chapter Twenty-Six

It was weird scanning a series of romantic poems for Lucas. A normal person would have just sent him the titles and told him to Google them. But since when was I normal?

I sent the files without making any comments about them. I'd written my reactions for Mrs. Lowenstein, but like I'd told Lucas in my earlier email they hadn't been my real reactions. However, I hadn't been completely honest about what my true reactions were to him either. Rather than admitting that every cheesy line made me think about him and caused my heart to bleed in a truly pathetic way, I'd made some jokes about how lame the words were and how ridiculous poetry is in general. It was better that way.

The twins were outside again, but I didn't feel like playing in the snow. Not now that Lucas had mentioned snowmen. Instead, I crashed on the couch beside Kevin. He was playing hockey this time and I watched him, waiting until he'd finished his game before asking if I could play.

He sighed. "You really want to play?"

I nodded, controller already primed.

He didn't look like he believed me, but he exited his league and started a match for us. I noticed that he took the weakest rated team while giving me the strongest one, but I didn't say anything about it.

It was a slaughter. I was down by eight at the end of the first period. Eight!

Kev tossed his controller down beside him. "If we talk about whatever's bothering you, can things go back to normal?"

I ran my fingers down the side of my controller, looking at the TV even though the pause screen was up. "Nothing's wrong. I'm just bored."

"Dude. I'm your brother, not an idiot."

I cocked my head to the side. "Those aren't mutually exclusive."

He knocked his knee into mine. "I'm the one wiping the ice with your ass. If there's an idiot here, it's not me."

"Whatever." I made sure my fingers were in the right spots over the buttons. "Let's go. Next period's mine."

He grunted at me like he was annoyed, but picked up his controller and started the game again.

I did better in the second period. He only scored five.

"Seriously," he said as the puck dropped to start the third. "Is it that Hunter guy? Cause I can beat the shit out of him if you want."

"No you couldn't." Pressing buttons like crazy, I managed to deflect a shot from him and actually get my guys to take the puck to his side of the ice.

"Wanna bet?" He whistled as I came closer to scoring than I had all game. "The guy's a total pansy."

"The guy's got like half a foot and fifty pounds on you, kid."

Kev snorted. "He's not that much bigger than me."

One eye still on the game, I stole a quick glance at my brother. He wasn't much smaller than Hunter at all. It was just that even with my brother beside me I had trouble thinking of him as anything other than the sniveling little brat he used to be. "No, I guess not. It isn't him though."

"Ah!" He grinned at me. "See! There is something wrong with you! Knew it!"

I used his distraction to send a slap shot straight into the back of his goal. "Hah!"

He rolled his eyes. "One point. I'm still winning by like a million."

"By twelve. That's a mere dozen, brother mine."

"Might as well be a million," he said. But he watched the screen after that.

Neither of us scored again. "Rematch?" I asked.

He looked at me for a little while. "Yeah, alright. If you tell me what's wrong."

I sighed. "Do you want to talk about Lisa?"

"Lisa?"

I met his eyes. "Yeah. Cute girl. About five-five. Blonde. Curls with me."

He frowned and picked up the controller, restarting the game without any further attempts at getting me to open up.

A SENTIMENTAL POEM

by Darcy Bennet

There's a boy
There's always a boy
This boy, my boy...
He's just a boy
A boy with eyes
(eyes like gates to my soul)
A boy with hair
(hair like softest comfort)
A boy with a laugh
(a laugh like a kiss from God)
A boy who I could have had
Maybe
When I was too stupid to see
A boy who doesn't want me now
For sure
When I'm too stupid to look away

Chapter Twenty-Seven

To everyone's disappointment, school was in session Wednesday morning after a two hour delay. The students weren't the only ones grumbling, either. I overheard a bunch of teachers moaning about how hard delayed days were with trying to cram all the classes into a shortened schedule and how much they'd have rather have just stayed home.

Lucas sat beside me in English. It was the class we met in, the one in which we had that fateful discussion about how much he didn't want to curl, the conversation I was now certain I'd completely misunderstood.

Despite being the one teacher to send out assignments via email, Mrs. Lowenstein seemed even less enthused about being at school than everyone else.

"So how many of you did the assignment?" she asked.

Not very many hands went up, making me feel like a complete freak for doing it as soon as it came in. Beside me, Lucas shifted uncomfortably. I raised my eyebrows at him. I'd sent him the materials, why hadn't he done the work? I looked away as my mind started to make suggestions, suggestions involving my best friend.

Mrs. Lowenstein sighed and muttered something that sounded like Yiddish. "You have ten minutes."

She sat down and opened a novel as around the room people dragged out their English books. The assignment was more than ten minutes long, but we only had twenty before lunch.

Not needing to cram on my homework, I followed Mrs. Lowenstein's lead and took out the book I was reading, even though I hadn't been paying enough attention to the first fifty pages to really know what the book was about beyond it being something concerning werewolves.

The metal tips of Lucas's chair legs squeaked against the floor, but I didn't look at him until he kicked his foot against the basket under my seat. "Hey, Darcy. Thanks for the materials yesterday. I got that part done."

His smile was rueful, or maybe embarrassed.

My thumbs pressed into the novel as I tried to stay calm. I wasn't sure what I felt... Attraction? Depression? Frustration? Whatever it was, it wasn't fun.

The skin around his eyes crinkled at my expression. "You okay?"

My eyes went back to the book, though the words on the page may as well have been written in Cyrillic. "Yeah, I'm fine. I did my homework."

His chair creaked again. I was starting to worry about it falling apart. "I'm not really a poet."

"Me neither." I turned the page, unread. "My poem sucks. I don't think it matters. Just write something."

There was a swoosh of paper, like he'd opened a notebook. "Don't suppose you'd let me see yours. You know, as a guide."

"Yeah. No." He was pretty much the last person I'd show that poem to. If Mrs. Lowenstein was one of those people who read student work out loud, she wouldn't even be getting a copy. "Just pattern it off something in the book."

"Okay..." He tapped the end of his pen against the notebook. I grit my teeth and fought down the urge to yank it out of his hand.

The girl in front of him turned around. "You could read my poem."

He smiled at her. "Thanks. But I think I've got it now."

She shrugged and gave me a funny look. What was up with that? Rebecca Townsend had said maybe three words to either

195

of us all year. Sure, she was a cheerleader and Lucas was on a school-sponsored sports team, but the squad didn't pay much attention to the hockey team. The hockey team sucked too bad.

A look of intensity lighting his face, Lucas scrawled something and I tried not to watch him. I wanted to know what he was writing, but was neither brave nor rude enough to scoot over and see. It made me wish I had something I was willing to share with him, so I'd have an excuse.

Yet when he finished and looked over and nudged the page toward me, I pretended not to see. I stared at the novel, acted like it was my world. I turned another page. I still hadn't read a word.

Chapter Twenty-Eight

The call had gone out right after school ended. We were playing an abridged playoff to determine who won the bonspiel and would go to Regionals. One more round to qualify to play for top position, then the title games.

The match-ups were on the board by the door and I smiled when I saw mine. It looked like an easy kill.

A cold blast of air hit my back as a group came in behind me. Amelia's voice overflowed excitement as she chattered. Was Lucas with her?

"Do you think you'll win?" she asked me, grabbing my hand in hers. Her fingers were sticky with something. That was okay though, big sisters can handle that sort of thing.

I smiled down at her. "I'm going to try."

"Well..." Hunter came up on my other side to read the board. "You'll make it to the final game."

I gave him a tilted look and he shrugged, not willing to commit past that. Whatever. Like I cared how he rated my chances.

No one questioned if Hunter would make it to the first place match or not. He would. He'd probably take it too.

A hand fell on my shoulder, the shoulder next to Amelia. But it wasn't her hand. It was Lucas's. "You'll do great," he said.

I smiled as the warmth from his hand spread throughout my body. "Thanks."

He squeezed and let go. I tried not to look too disappointed.

The door opened again and I started to feel a little trapped until Amelia tugged on my hand and urged me to move. "Come see something!"

"Amelia," Lucas said, drawing the name out in disapproval.

"What is it?" I asked. I gave her a huge smile and glanced at Lucas as she tugged me into a slow walk. He shook his head and followed us while Hunter stayed to talk to Ellen, who'd just come in. I wondered if he'd tell her she'd take the championship, but then reminded myself I didn't care.

People had been trickling in for a while and most of them congregated near the refreshments. I would have avoided the area, but Amelia pulled me straight through the congestion. My eyes caught on a plate of cupcakes as we passed. I hadn't eaten since lunch and I didn't eat too much then because I'd been hiding in the library, pretending I had work to do because I just didn't feel like talking to anyone and didn't want my friends figuring out that something was wrong. I mean, if it was obvious to Kevin, Jean would be able to tell in about thirty seconds.

Lucas scooped up one of the cupcakes and handed it to me. "They'll be gone before you're done."

"True. Thanks." I peeled back a little of the paper and took a nibble of the awesome sweetness. Oh, God, that was good. Dolores Reynolds must have made them. Her cupcakes were a source of pride for the whole town. "You have to get one of these, Lucas. They're amazing."

He smiled, his eyes flickering to my hand like maybe he'd just take some of mine.

I held it out. "Try it if you don't believe me."

My heart just about stopped when he leaned over and actually did it.

His eyes came up to mine as he straightened. "It's good."

Amelia yanked on my other hand, reminding me we'd stopped moving. "He can get his own. Come on!"

The bite I'd eaten rolled around in my stomach like crazy as I started walking again. I made myself take another nibble, mostly as an excuse not to say anything. I tried not to let myself think too much about how Lucas's lips touched the same section of cake just seconds before.

The hall to the club offices had been taken over by splashes of color courtesy of bright crayons and a curling themed coloring book. Amelia took us most of the way down the wall before stopping to point at one. "That's you!"

I smiled at the picture. It was a boy guiding a rock out of the hack, but it was a boy with hair like mine and Amelia had given him a pink shirt and a penguin necklace. "I love it."

There were some stick figures standing around behind the curler. The smallest one had long hair and a skirt. I touched the little figure. "Is that you?"

"Yep!" She grinned. "That's me. And that's Uncle Lulu. And that's my mom."

I put an arm around her and gave her a half-hug. "That is so awesome."

My eyes went to Lucas, but he wasn't watching me. He looked at the picture with a strange and unreadable expression on his face.

"Darcy?" Amelia asked. "Do you think when I'm older I can play on your team?"

Smiling, I nodded. "Sure. But you have to be thirteen to play in juniors and by then I'll be too old, so we'll have to wait until you're old enough for a grownup team."

"Oh." She frowned a little. "Okay. What about Lucas? Can he be on our team?"

I glanced at him. He was still looking at the artwork. "If he wants to be."

"But not Hunter," Amelia said. "Hunter's too bossy."

Lucas ruffled her hair. "Look who's talking. You know she's planning to skip this imaginary team of hers, right, Darcy?"

"Well, she'd have to be better at it than I am."

His eyebrows drew together. "No poisoning yourself like that."

"Poisoning?" Amelia squeaked, her eyes getting big.

"He means mentally," I told her. "In my thoughts. What's

that quote? Whether you think you can do something or think you can't, you're right?"

"Exactly," said Lucas.

My phone started chiming. It was my warning to make sure I was ready to go. I wasn't. I needed shoes and a lot more confidence. The shoes I could do something about.

I got them on quickly and went to meet my team out on the ice. It looked like Hunter was one sheet over from me again. It wasn't statistically odd since we only had four sheets to play on, but it seemed like it was happening too often. He grabbed me as I passed him, his arm latching around my waist to hold me in place. "Good luck."

Even as I gave him a tight smile, I tried to squirm out of his grasp. The cupcake from before was doing jumping jacks inside me, threatening to come up all over Hunter's smarmy self. But I couldn't let that happen. For one thing, it would be embarrassing. And for a more important thing, it would be bad for the ice.

"Can we talk after?"

"Sure," I said, hoping it would make him let go of me. It didn't. Would I have to say something to draw attention to us? Because if I started screaming, he'd be fending off broom hits in no time.

"I got some tickets," he said, not seeming to have any clue how much I wanted to leave. "Broadway."

He followed the statement up with a look like he expected me to throw myself on him in gratitude. Yeah, right. Like I'd whore myself out for a seat at a random Broadway production. It probably wasn't even a good show or he would have said what it was.

I wrenched away and this time he let me, either because it finally dawned on him that he needed to or because he was finished and moving on to curling now.

My teammates stared at me when I got to them.

"Not a word," I said.

They looked at each other, but kept quiet until they started wishing the other team good curling.

The game was close, closer than it should have been. And long. I kept second-guessing myself and spent way too much time on calling shots. Then the other games all ended before us, which, of course, made things worse because I knew everyone was watching me. Even though they probably weren't. Probably most people were eating or drinking or watching the NHL game on the TV upstairs.

It came down to the last shot of the last end. It was mine.

I looked down the ice and took a long breath. Was I going to be right about thinking I could do it or about thinking I couldn't? I fought the urge to look for Lucas. He didn't have anything to do with this. My mind flashed on Amelia's face. She believed in me. Unlikely as it seemed, to that little girl I was a hero. Heroes make their shots.

I twisted the rock on its side, wiped off the dirt that may or may not have been clinging to it, and nodded to myself.

I could do this.

Eyes locked onto Maria's broom, I lined up in the hack. Slid out... Glided... Released the rock...

Too light!

Shit!

"Hard!" I yelled.

My sweepers brought their brooms down, sweeping fast and furious. The game depended on this shot. I'd messed it up, but maybe my girls could save us.

"Hurry!" I bellowed. "Hard!"

It was a prayer more than a command.

There are people who say good sweepers make a team. I was suddenly one of them.

They swept that damn rock for all they were worth.

"All the way!" Maria yelled, coming down to sweep with them.

And together they saved my horrible, no good throw. They bought it the extra feet it needed, took it right up to the rock it had to hit.

And there was our last shot. Frozen dead-center on the button.

My whole body sagged with the relief of it.

The opposing skip whistled. "That was some good sweeping."

I smiled at her. "Yeah, they just saved my ass."

She nodded in agreement, then held her hand out to shake. "Good game, Bennet."

"Thanks." I shook. "Good game. You made us earn that."

Shaking done, we cleaned our ice. My blood was whirling in my ears and I could swear I was still tasting cupcake in the back of my throat. "Good game, you guys. Thanks for saving me."

"Nah," Lisa said, shaking her head as she swept the debris we'd gathered into a dustpan. "You would have thrown it harder if you didn't know we could do it. You just wanted us to feel needed."

I laughed and took the pan from her to dump it in the little bin by the water cooler. "Yeah. I'm really caring like that."

We were all smiling as we went into the warm room.

My smile didn't last long.

The others all went upstairs to look for food. The crew was already getting the ice ready for the next game, so we didn't have much time to find sustenance before having to face off against Ellen again.

Me, I needed the bathroom.

That part went alright, but when I came out and was punched in the gut. Metaphorically speaking.

Even though his back was to me, I recognized Lucas first. In part, it was because his build was engraved in my mind. In part, it was the hair I wanted to reach out and touch. And in part it was because he was the one talking.

Adam was beside him. His eyes went wide when he saw me and he started waving his hands, gesturing for Lucas to shut up. But Lucas didn't figure out what he was saying in time.

"Come on," Lucas told Hunter, "the only reason you'd possibly want to go out with someone like Darcy Bennet is-"

He cut off in sudden horror as he caught me with the corner of his eye. Paling, he turned his head toward me, stricken silent.

Hunter chuckled. "Oh, go on. By all means, finish that sentence."

Lucas's lips parted, but he didn't say anything as his eyes roved frantically over my face.

"Don't bother," I said.

Chapter Twenty-Nine

The bathroom door banged shut behind me and I thumped my fists down beside the sink. My vision shimmered as I glared at myself in the mirror. I wasn't going to cry. He hadn't hurt me. I was just pissed off that I'd wasted so much energy obsessing over him.

The door opened again and I plastered a bored look on my face. It fell off the second the newcomer's reflection came into view.

Lucas looked bad. Like gum that had been stuck on a shoe all day. Like misery incarnate. Frankly, like complete shit.

Good.

"Darcy..." he said, his voice catching.

I closed my eyes and counted to three. "You're not supposed to be in here."

"I'll risk the arrest record."

My lips curled ever so slightly.

There was a breeze as he moved and when he spoke again, his voice was right beside me like he was leaning against the counter. "You weren't supposed to hear that."

My eyes opened so I could stare at him. "No kidding."

He winced. "That's not what I meant."

"Really?" I straightened and folded my arms across my stomach. "So you weren't trying to say that I wasn't supposed to know you were dissing me behind my back?"

"I wasn't—" He cut off with a growl of frustration. His

hands gripped the edge of the vanity with enough force to turn his knuckles white and he trembled as he looked at me. He took a long breath which seemed to do nothing to calm him. "Darcy, I wasn't dissing you. I would never do that."

I dropped my eyes to the floor, unable to keep looking at him. "Sure you wouldn't."

He pushed away from the counter and walked toward me, backing me up until I hit the wall and couldn't go any further. I stared at his chest and reminded myself that being so close to him did absolutely nothing for me.

"Look at me?" he whispered. "Please?"

I shut my eyes.

His sigh brushed over my hair and made my treacherous heart beat faster.

The door opened again and new steps approached. There was a whimper and then a weak female voice complaining, "This is the women's bathroom."

"Sorry," Lucas murmured.

But he didn't leave after she walked around us and into one of the stalls.

We were all quiet as time lagged on. Then the girl spoke again. I recognized her voice now. It was Hiro of Team Nemesis. Lovely. "Guys, I can't pee with you out there. Seriously. Go somewhere else. Please?"

"Darcy?" Lucas asked.

I shook my head.

"Alright." He moved away and I started to shiver, as though I'd been warming myself with him. Which was ridiculous. "But... What I was saying... What I was saying was that he only wanted you because I did first. He has a history of it. Every time I look at a girl for more than five seconds, he swoops in. And any time I really, seriously, like her... It's like a personal challenge for him. And he'll take it up no matter what, even if he's dating someone else already. Which he is. I don't know if you know that, but Ellen's in his apartment as many nights as not. But in your case, what I was saying was stupid. Because there are a million reasons for a guy to want you."

My eyes opened, but he was already out the door.

Had he just said what I thought he did?

But... I shouldn't read too much into it, right? I mean, I'd already suspected he might have liked me a little at one point. That didn't change the fact that his affections had moved on. Right? I mean, it's not like he claimed Hunter was interested in me now because he still wanted me. He'd merely confirmed that he used to.

But... He confirmed that he used to. And he begged me to look at him. And he looked so miserable and lost and beyond hope...

"Darcy?" Hiro said from her stall. "I don't think Carol would want me to say this, but if you don't go after him, you're an idiot."

A second later, I bolted through the door.

I was too late. Lucas wasn't anywhere.

Jean rushed up to me. "He went to his car. What did you say to him? He looked crazy."

I shook my head. "I... I said the wrong thing. Like usual."

"Oh, sweetie." She hugged me, but I didn't hug back because I was too busy looking at the exit. I couldn't go out in these shoes. But by the time I changed, he'd be long gone.

I pulled away from Jean and started unlacing a shoe, my balance wobbling and my fingers clumsy.

"I'm sure it's okay," Jean said. "I mean, he's obviously crazy about you."

My foot crashed onto the ground and I nearly toppled over. "No, he's crazy about you. Why am I doing this?"

I stared down at my untied shoe. Was I really about to race out into the parking lot in my socks chasing after some guy who'd been hitting on my best friend all week? Just because he'd said he used to be attracted to me and looked upset that I might think he hated me?

"Me?" Jean laughed. "What gave you that idea?"

I bent over and started to retie my shoe. She didn't know he'd gotten in the way when she'd been trying to hook up with Adam. She didn't know about Lisa's little adventure. "I have my reasons."

"Well, they're wrong."

There were tears in my eyes, so I stayed down even after I got my knot tied.

"Darcy," Jean knelt down in front of me, took my chin in her hand, and tipped my face up so she could meet my eyes. "I've been hanging out with Lucas because we became friends after he helped me get Adam. You remember Adam? That really hot guy over by the glass? The one I've been chasing all semester?"

"You broke up with him."

She moved her hand to rest against my forehead, like she was checking to see if I had a fever. "Are you delirious or something? I most certainly did not break up with Adam. I am very happy with Adam."

"But Carol said..." I groaned.

She nodded in sympathy. "If Carol said we split up, she lied. And if she's the one who gave you this stupid idea that Lucas is into me, she lied. Probably because she hoped you'd do something stupid enough that he'd give up on you and move on to her."

Something stupid like throw myself at Hunter. That's why she'd said all that stuff about our "chemistry" and how we belonged together. It was a setup. Maybe...

Jean brushed my hair back from my face. "Lucas helped me with Adam. We're friends. That's it."

"But..." I shook my head. "He didn't help..."

"Yes, he did." Her words were short, precisely formed. Even if I hadn't known her all my life, I would have believed her. "He told me about your little agreement, remember? Then he said he was sorry and he went and told Adam he'd been wrong, told him he needed to take me to the Waltz. If you want to blame him for me having a date and thus going to the dance and thus going to the after party and becoming acquainted with the police force, that's fine. But he's the reason I'm with Adam. Which I am, if you missed that memo. We're here together right now."

I frowned at the carpet. I wanted to believe her, I really did.

But I wanted it too much, so I was scared of fooling myself and I kept arguing. "He hated the idea of you and Adam."

"Yes." She smiled slightly and shrugged. "He thought Adam was trying to take advantage of me. Kinda sweet, if misguided. And he probably didn't think he'd stand much a shot with you if he let his best friend break your best friend's heart. When he figured out he was wrong and Adam wasn't just playing with me, he fixed things."

"But..."

"When Maria wasn't here Saturday, what did he do?"

I swallowed. "He went to get her. But—"

"And when my idiot sister needed a ride from freaking Poughkeepsie, what did he do then?"

"You're not... How did...?"

She grinned. "I have my sources. Answer my question."

"He went to get her," I said. "But—"

"Why?"

I fell back on my butt and sat staring at her. "Because he was worried about her? Because she's your sister?"

Jean shook her head and crawled closer. "Poor, silly, Darcy. No. He went because she's your friend."

My eyes searched her face, looking for any of the tells that would say she was lying. She wasn't. But that still left the possibility of her being wrong. "Did he tell you that?"

She sighed. "No, he didn't. But, Darce, it's obvious!"

"No. It isn't."

Her head turned to the side and she shrugged. "Well, he came back. Ask him."

She stood up and waited until he saw her to say, "Good curling, Darcy. I'll see you after the game."

I drew my knees up against the urge to spring up and run. I might have given into it if I'd had any idea which direction I wanted to go. But I didn't.

Lucas paused when he crossed paths with Jean. She said something and I lowered my head to keep from seeing what he did in response.

I was still looking down, studying the weave of my pants

208

when he sat beside me.

He was close. Almost touching. I wanted to move closer. And I wanted to sprint away.

He cleared his throat. "She says you think I spent all night fetching Lisa for my health."

I turned my head away. "No. I don't think that."

"But you don't know why I did it."

Blinking back tears, I promised to kill Jean next time I saw her.

"It was your expression," he said. "I couldn't stand to see you looking like that. Not if I could do anything to stop it."

There was a crinkling sound and then a folded piece of paper appeared in my line of vision.

"I wrote this," he said. "In English. I'd already written one to turn in. I wrote this one for you, that's why I tried to get you to look at it then. It's a little melodramatic. Sorry."

Not taking the paper, I turned to stare at him. He was so, so close... His eyes were locked on me like I was the only thing in the world, like we weren't sitting on the edge of a milling crowd. Like he couldn't hear the man making announcements, saying that they were ready to start the next set of games now.

"Please?" he asked, moving the paper back into my line of sight.

I took it without breaking eye contact. "Will I like it?"

"I don't know."

We stared at each other, neither daring to move. Even breathing seemed too likely to break the spell.

Someone kicked me.

I looked up to see Carol glaring at me like I was queen of all that's evil. "If you're not on the ice in one minute, we get a point and credit for the first end."

Slowly, Lucas stood up. He seemed even taller than usual as he looked down on his friend's sister. If he knew that she hated me talking to him because she was crushing on him herself, he showed no sympathy for it as he held a hand down to draw me to my feet.

Words For Her

by Lucas Fitzwilliam

Can she not hear my words?
Am I saying them wrong?
Should I keep on trying?
Or do I just not belong
with her?

When she's around
Nothing goes the right way.
I just don't have a gift
For the right thing to say
to her.

I'd give up my soul,
Give all that I own.
I'd say or do anything
To not be alone,
without her.

She's right there beside me.
She's reading a book.
But she won't turn my way,
Won't spare even one look
for me.

Chapter Thirty

I read the poem Lucas had given me on my way out to the ice. Analytically speaking, even though it was better than mine, it probably wasn't the best poem ever written. However, if the point of poetry is to elicit an emotional response, then he was a master of the form.

Ellen sneered at me when I went to shake her hand. "In tears already? You haven't lost yet."

I smiled at her. "I already won."

She rolled her eyes. "Yeah, well, let's see about that. Good curling."

"Good curling," I said, and actually meant it.

I even meant it when I said it to Carol. I felt a little sorry for her. It wasn't her fault we liked the same boy. Or that the boy liked me better. Yeah, okay, she was a lying bitch, but she was going to be a lonely lying bitch, because Lucas was mine. Mine!

The happy mood stayed through the first two shooters from each team, but when I was calling Maria's shot, I looked upstairs and noticed something.

Lucas was there. I'd known he was, but I hadn't seen him before. He leaned against the wall, near the front, but not so near that people hadn't been getting in the way of me seeing him until then.

He stood beside Jean and Adam, who may have been pulling for different teams but were still plastered to each other in a way that made me feel like even more of a moron for thinking she had something going with Lucas. But Lucas didn't look happy. His shoulders were slumped, his head bent too much. He looked... sad? Why?

Frowning at him, I completely missed it when Maria made her shot. By the time I realized the rock was coming toward me, I'd already messed up calling its line. It was curling wrong, because I hadn't told the sweepers to sweep when I should have.

Ellen smirked. "You may want to try waking up, Darcy."

I tried to shake it off and pay more attention. I did. But my eyes kept going to Lucas.

And I realized... I hadn't said anything to him about how I felt. He had no idea I was curling on air because of him. He had no idea what was going on in my head.

The instant our stone went still I rushed down the ice.

I passed Maria with a, "Be right back!" and jumped off the ice to hurry along the carpet on my way to the warm room.

Hunter tried to stop me. "Where are you going?"

I kept going without answering and he didn't stop his game to follow me.

As my foot hit the first step, Lucas appeared at the top of the flight, asking almost the same question. "What are you doing?"

I sprinted up to him. "You're too tall!"

"Um... Sorry?"

He watched me, his lips dancing with amusement as I edged around him to go up one step higher.

"That's better," I said.

"Okay."

He stared at me like he had no idea what was expected of him.

I shook my head. "You really do have horrible social skills."

He opened his mouth, probably to say he was sorry again, but I didn't have time to spend on things like that. I threw my arms around his neck and kissed him like our lives depended on it.

His breath was jagged when I pulled away.

I smiled as my hand played in his hair, which was every bit as soft as it looked. "I was just pretending to read. I was really watching you the entire time."

He laughed and I had to kiss him again.

"Darcy?"

"Yeah?"

His fingers traced along my jaw. "You're in the middle of a curling match."

"Oh. Right."

He wrapped his arms around me and turned, placing me down again on the step beneath him. He bent and brushed his lips against mine. "Beat them, okay? Then we'll talk some more."

"Okay." I grinned as I took the stairs backward so I could watch him as I went down them. "As long as by talk you mean make out in stairwells."

He laughed. "I'll make a list of all the stairwells in Meryton."

The girls had been waiting and when I got back they all wanted to know why.

I grinned at them. "I had something more important to do. Let's curl!"

All of them, both teams, stared at me.

Lisa stood next to me as I wiped off my rock. "What could be more important to Darcy Bennet than curling?"

As I lined up for my throw, I smiled mysteriously.

Cat laughed. "Must be love."

I couldn't argue, but I could send a perfect shot down the ice.

It was one of my better games. Not because I'd suddenly decided I liked skipping. Not because I managed to make most my shots. And not just because I beat Team Nemesis by a score of eight to six.

It was one of my better games because I wasn't worried about what would happen next. I wasn't thinking about getting into Regionals. I wasn't thinking about Nationals or Worlds. I wasn't worried about what would happen next year, when I'd be on a team without Jean, grounded or not, for the first time in my life. I was thinking about having some fun, then dragging a certain someone into a stairwell so I could have even more.

Which is exactly what I did.

WINTER BREAK TO-DO LIST

1. Prep for REGIONALS!

2. Lure Lucas into stairwells.

3. Talk Jean's mom into letting Jean curl in Regionals so I don't have to skip.

5. Find Lucas an awesome Christmas present. (He already gave me an adorable little penguin charm to put on my zipper for luck at Regionals. And he says he's getting me something else too since he couldn't wait to give me that one!)

6. Start English research project on the early history of curling.

7. Play with the half-monsters so Mom can get some rest.

8. More prepping for Regionals.

9. Much more hanging out in stairwells with my incredibly awesome boyfriend.

Acknowledgements

Yeah, this is the part where I tell you what you already know. Namely, it takes more than just an author to make a book. It takes family, friends, readers, and, of course, cats.

Okay, my cats didn't help much, other than by offering me endless affection and cuddles. But I might not have made it without them. So, special kudos to my kitties, along with my Kickstarter backers for their support, Jane Austen for writing the original Pride and Prejudice, my fellow Granite Curling Club members for taking me into the sport, and everyone everywhere who ever said some variant of, "A curling novel? Cool!"

I definitely couldn't have written this novel without the support of my beloved, Jimmy, who has always believed in me more than I believe in myself. Thanks for that. And thanks for driving me around for hours every Friday so I can curl.

My son, Eric, would tell you he had nothing to do with this, but he's always been one of my most dedicated fans (even though he doesn't enjoy romances or curling) and has most certainly made the many sacrifices all children of writers have to make. You make me a better me, kiddo.

Special thanks also belongs to Elle Lebeau, an awesome curler and a great friend. She's not only my go-to-girl for curling details, but her enthusiasm for my early drafts carried me through revisions. She was also one of my leading Kickstarter backers, but I was totally planning to fawn over her anyway. This book wouldn't have been nearly as strong without her.

Thanks also to the amazing Cassandra Marshall, not just for being a top-notch editor and cover designer, but for her incredible feedback as a beta-reader and her general enthusiasm for this book from the outline stage.

And, of course, no acknowledgement section is complete without a shout-out to the author's parents. Mom, Dad, thank you for decades of support and adoration. I love you guys.

Made in the USA
San Bernardino, CA
07 December 2015